How to
Marry a Country
Music Star

CATHRYN BROWN

Sienna Bay Press

PO Box 158582

Nashville, Tennessee 37215

www.cathrynbrown.com

Cover designed by Najla Qamber Designs

(www.najlaqamberdesigns.com)

ISBN: 978-1-945527-48-7

How to Marry a Country Music Star/Cathryn Brown—1st ed.

❀ Created with Vellum

DEAR READER

Nashville, Tennessee, is a fun place to live. Music lives and breathes in its soul. That sounds dramatic, but it's true. You may see a musician playing in a parking lot in the suburbs or on a city sidewalk.

I always want to make sure I get things right, so I interviewed musicians. One in particular shared so many details that it helped bring more life to the story.

The book opens at Carly Daniels' mansion. She's a country music star who has fallen on hard times. The mansion is one I patterned after the former home of a music star that I actually toured. It's no longer there in real life, but it lives on in How to Marry a Country Music Star.

The Ryman Auditorium, the Parthenon, and many other Nashville locations are real and still exist.

I hope you enjoy Carly and Jake's story, which doesn't end when this book does. Their wedding is in Runaway to Romance.

CHAPTER ONE

*C*arly Daniels looked up at the mansion in front of her. She may have been born in California, but in her heart, she would always be a Tennessee girl. Nothing, and she meant *nothing*, had been a bigger fantasy than a Southern *Gone with the Wind* mansion with three-story columns and a wide front porch.

"Are you ready to go, Carly?" Maggie Morales, her best friend since the third grade, called from that front porch.

Carly sighed. "I don't have a choice. I've lost the house. Lost *everything*."

Maggie walked down the steps to Carly, and put an arm over her shoulders. "Move out to Seattle, live in my guest room, get a fresh start away from the music industry."

"My adult life has been shaped by the music I sing, and by Nashville. I can't imagine living anywhere else or doing anything else."

Maggie hugged her. "Know that you are always welcome. I'll send you a plane ticket at a moment's notice."

Carly hugged her back. "Thank you." Then she stepped

back and started for the house. "I'd like one last look at Plantation Daniels. A lot of great memories were made in this house." She choked back a sob. "Before TJ took it all."

Maggie hurried to catch up with her. "Remember, no bitterness."

"Ha! That's easy for you to say. He didn't steal everything you owned."

Maggie muttered something.

"What?"

Her friend cleared her throat. "I said that if you'd let me read your contracts, none of this would have happened."

Carly stayed silent as they went back inside. Climbing the grand curving staircase to the second floor, she noticed the faint shadows on the wall to her left, the only clues that her gold records—sold at auction—once hung there.

At the landing, she said, "I didn't want to bother you. TJ came highly recommended as a financial manager in the music industry, and he seemed trustworthy."

Maggie snorted.

"Now who's got a negative attitude?" Carly went into her now empty bedroom with her friend following behind.

Maggie said, "Sorry," but her tone told Carly she would punch TJ if he ever showed his face again.

Carly took the stairs tucked in the corner, the ones that went up to the attic, the room she had most enjoyed. Her closet.

Magazine editors loved to show photos of her massive closet. What they didn't seem to realize was that the costumes, other clothes, and accessories that went along with being a country music star took up a lot of space.

The clothes that hadn't sold at auction lay piled in the middle of the floor, waiting to be hauled away. The house had been repossessed by the bank, and everything in it sold to pay debts she hadn't known about.

There had been takers for some of her more glamorous costumes, but not for most of the rest of the clothes. And hats. And boots.

She'd been told she could take anything that hadn't sold, but she didn't have any use for a sequined dress. All dressed up and nowhere to go. Pathetic.

Maggie dug through the pile and held up a black dress. "This is cute."

"What do I need with a little black dress? Elegant restaurants are out. I can barely afford fast food."

"Take it. Just in case your life gets better. Or you move to Seattle." Maggie gave her a look that said she hadn't dropped that idea, then reached for a sparkly evening bag. "This too."

A pair of hot pink cowboy boots sat on a shelf, lined up with other boots. Carly went over and grabbed them. "I've always loved these. And a girl can always use a pair of pink boots."

"Now you're talking."

With the dress over one arm and the boots tucked under the other with the evening bag stuffed inside one, Carly spun on her heels and hurried down the stairs to the second-floor landing. "I always loved trying out new songs from this spot. The acoustics are amazing. On some not-so-great days, I'd stand here and sing 'Sunshine Cowboy.' I've sung it a thousand times in venues around the globe, but that song always cheers me up."

"You and all of your fans." Maggie rubbed Carly's arm. "Sing it one more time."

Carly took a deep breath and started singing the words that had made her a household name when she was eighteen.

Country songs could be sad, but this one was pure happiness. She choked a little on the third verse but made it to the end with tears streaming down her face.

She scrubbed her cheeks with her hands. "Lessons learned. Write happy songs and have a lawyer read everything before you sign it."

Maggie hugged her again. "You're a fighter. You may have some struggles, but you'll come out a winner."

Head held high, Carly went down the rest of the stairs with her friend beside her. She picked up her guitar case with her favorite guitar inside from where it rested beside the door. "At least this was in my name. I just wish I wanted to play it. TJ seems to have stolen that too." Money and dreams had vanished over night.

Once outside the door, Carly turned and locked it. Whoever owned the property now would have a key. She set the guitar in the rusty bed of her truck beside the three boxes that contained her worldly possessions.

"I wish you'd had the red sports car in your name," Maggie said as she cautiously stepped into the truck. "I can't even tell the original color of this thing."

The driver's door groaned as Carly tugged it open. "Just be glad I paid cash for a vehicle my groundskeeper could use around the property. It wasn't part of the TJ mess." As she climbed inside, she set the dress and boots beside her.

"Rusty with a hole in the seat . . . and loud," Maggie said as Carly turned the key and started it up.

Carly gave her a mock glare. "You'd better be nice. It's about a forty-five-minute drive in this truck or a much longer walk from Arrington to Nashville International Airport."

Maggie held up her hands and added, "I'm glad. I'm very glad."

Carly started down the long winding drive to the highway, curving through several hundred acres of green, rolling hills she used to own. On the last curve, she glanced in the rearview mirror and saw the house for a moment. Then it was gone forever.

She'd trusted people with her career. She'd had to, especially when she was starting out. She should have known better than to trust someone to manage all of her money. But she hadn't been the only musician to get cleaned out by TJ.

They drove in silence until Maggie nudged her. "You've been closemouthed about your plans. Except that you won't let me help you."

"I have money." She didn't add that it was only enough to live cheaply for a month. "My grandmother left me some a few years ago, and I didn't have the heart to spend it. That account wasn't connected to TJ."

"And with that you'll . . .?"

"I made a motel reservation." She didn't add that she'd discovered the money wouldn't cover apartment rental and a security deposit.

"I'm guessing you won't be staying downtown at the Hermitage Hotel."

Carly shook her head. "Good guess. No, I won't be at a five-star hotel with rose petals in the bath."

She put on her turn signal to enter the airport ramp off the interstate. "It's the Music Inn. I stayed there when I moved to Nashville. It was clean and quiet. I have a month to find a job and a place to live. To start over. Maybe find my music again."

"Sounds like a good plan. Text me every few days."

Maggie shook her finger at her. "Either I get updates or I'm coming back to check on you—with actual suitcases for you and a ticket to Seattle."

Carly grinned. Maggie had a way of making her smile even when she didn't feel like it, and that was the best kind of friend.

They came to a stop at the airport's loading zone, and as Carly stepped out, a woman pointed to her and said something to the man at her side. They hurried over and asked for her autograph. Carly smiled and signed her name.

Maggie joined her as the couple went inside the airport. "You said you wanted to start over. Can you? Carly Daniels is a well-known country music star."

"I've been hiding in my house since I learned about TJ's bad money management. Everything happened quickly, and I've been so stressed out that I haven't thought about any of this." She pictured life with the media hounding her to learn more about the former star. "I know I don't want reporters crowded around my motel room. That defeats the purpose of a fresh start, and other guests would be bothered."

"Maybe change your hair color?"

She held up a handful of her long, curly blonde hair. "I used to have brown, naturally wavy hair. My first manager thought I'd succeed better as a blonde." She studied the hair in her hand. "Maybe he was right, but I'm ready for a change. Besides, I can't pay my hair stylist anymore to keep it this color."

"And lose the curls. You spend way too much time on them."

"Good plan. While I'm at it, I'll cut it a bit shorter. Anything else, wise one, before you have to board your plane?"

"Makeup."

"Excuse me?" Carly raised one eyebrow. She'd spent over a half hour, maybe closer to forty-five minutes, on her makeup this morning.

"You created a curly-blonde, ton-of-makeup persona that isn't you."

Carly pictured herself. "I like it."

Maggie shook her head. "I think you've added another layer every year. This year, the eye shadow is heavy, the lip color is dark, and there's a slash of blush across each cheek."

Carly put her hand on the side of her face. "You've never mentioned it."

"You seemed happy. But now you want to change. I've spent a week with you and this," she gestured at Carly, "isn't who you are."

Carly blew out a deep breath and considered Maggie's words. "I think my makeup became part of a costume I wore every day."

"No one would expect to see you in more natural makeup."

A woman slowed and stared at Carly as she walked by, then smiled and nodded at her but kept going. Must be a Nashvillian. Locals often acknowledged stars with a nod but left them alone.

Carly tilted her head to one side as she pictured her new look. "So, Carly Daniels will become a wavy-haired brunette with somewhat shorter hair and natural makeup?"

Maggie grinned. "That's a great start." Her friend popped up the handle on her luggage. "Think about your name too. It doesn't matter how different you look if you follow that up with 'Hi, I'm Carly Daniels.'"

"My first manager gave me that name. He thought Carly

sounded music-worthy and that Daniels would be easier than McDaniel."

"Let me know what you decide." Maggie checked her watch. "It's almost boarding time." She gave Carly a big hug. "Take care of yourself." Then, with a sigh, she turned and wheeled her luggage toward the door.

"Back to Charlotte McDaniel?" Carly called after her.

"That's who you really are, anyway. Find Charlotte again." Maggie waved as she went inside.

Wiping away a few tears as she left the airport—how did you fill in the gap for your best friend?—Carly, no Charlotte, drove to her home for the next month. She had considered the options for her life and whittled them down to somewhere in the neighborhood of none.

She had a bank account balance less than many college freshmen, and just like them, had been living on the cheapest food she could find since all of this struck. Gone were the fresh fruit smoothies every morning and long lunches out with friends. Those *friends* had stopped calling once her star had fallen.

Of course, the news media had taken care of announcing her story to the world. And sales had crashed. According to them, she had spent every dollar on a wasted life that included illegal substances, which she had never consumed, and copious amounts of legal ones, which she rarely consumed. They had declared her a self-indulgent mess.

The problem was that someone else had been holding on to her money and her reputation, and they'd done a fine job of stealing one and trashing the other.

Once she had a regular paycheck, she hoped the security of it would give her creativity a boost so she'd want to write songs again. She had to find a way to make her comeback in country music.

But for now, she'd just be Charlotte McDaniel.

On the way to the Music Inn, she stopped at a drugstore to buy the materials for changing her identity. Then, with hair color, scissors, some softer eye makeup, blush, and lip color, and enough food for a couple of days, she pulled up to the inn. She stepped out of her truck and froze.

This couldn't be right. She turned to check the sign. It said Music Inn. In the last decade, her charming small motel had become a fleabag with peeling paint and trash on the ground. The two-story building had steps leading to a second story, with all the doors opening from the outside, and every inch of it in bad shape.

She took a deep breath, immediately regretting it. Stale smoke and other lovely scents she chose not to identify assaulted her nose. She turned to leave but stopped again.

Where to? She'd prepaid and doubted they would want to give her that money back. How bad could it be, anyway?

She entered the motel lobby—if one could use a grand term like that for a small room with a chipped counter and a floor that desperately needed new carpet. She walked up to the desk, and the older man behind it ignored her.

"Excuse me?"

He glanced up. "Yes?" he said, then blew out smoke from the cigar he had clenched between his teeth.

The excellent customer service she'd experienced before seemed to have left the building when the filth moved in.

"I'm here to check in."

He chuckled. "Carly Daniels, right?"

"Please correct my name to Charlotte McDaniel."

He erased her name in a ledger—apparently

computerized motel systems hadn't reached here—then wrote it in as she'd asked. He handed her a key. "Enjoy your stay." He followed that with evil laughter.

She hadn't needed to add creepy to her day. She'd lock her door tonight. Glancing back at him as she exited, she thought, *and shove something heavy in front of it.*

After unlocking her unit's door, she pushed it open. "No!" she cried. "I can't do this!" She hurried through the room to check the bathroom. At the far end of that room, mottled gray tiles lined the shower. Gray had become a popular color, so that was okay. A tentative step into the bathroom changed her mind. "Gray *grime. Everywhere.*" She stifled a scream.

Her options were . . . *zero.* She'd paid in advance. The manager's laugh had probably been for that reason.

She'd have to clean this dump. Her next stop would be back at the front office. They must have cleaning supplies, even if no one appeared to be using them.

CHAPTER TWO

*J*ake loosened his tie and shrugged out of his suit coat as he reached his car. A week of negotiations had secured a new commercial property to flip. But between that and having to push up his sleeves to help hang drywall at another site, he'd used up more than a day's energy. A quiet dinner and a swim in his pool called his name.

His phone rang, so he pulled it out of his coat pocket, hoping it wasn't another business call. The screen was lit up with his sister's photo.

He tapped the screen. "Lizzie! How are things in the world of real estate agents?"

He only heard slight static through the line.

"Lizzie?"

A sigh, perhaps the longest he'd ever heard, came across. "There's the smallest, tiniest, possibility that I did something monumentally stupid."

As he waited, knowing she'd keeping speaking without

encouragement from him, he unlocked his car and climbed in.

"Okay. It's majorly stupid. One of my clients *knew* he would buy a motel but didn't have the cash right away. Based on the square footage, it seemed like a steal. I thought, why not? I'd buy it, make a few updates, and flip it to him. He'd get a building that's in better shape, and I'd make a profit on it, so we'd both win."

"You walked through it first, right?"

More silence.

Steadying himself, he counted to ten. "Lizzie, you didn't buy it sight unseen, did you?"

"Of course not. But I was leaving town to meet with a decorating client, and I could only check it out online."

"I wouldn't have done that, but with photos and videos online, it worked, didn't it?"

"*No. It didn't.*" His tough-as-nails sister sounded near the edge. "I did a quick check. The photos looked good, and the agent had it set up to sign the agreement online."

"It needs a *little* work?" He prayed that was all. His sister had a knack for buying real estate and selling it for a lot more than she'd paid.

She shouted, "It needs a bulldozer!"

"It can't be that bad."

Silence greeted him.

Lizzie sighed. "I checked reviews on travel sites this morning. I quote, 'Vacation getaway for entomologists.' That's an insect—"

"I know. An insect scientist." He cringed. Anything but bugs. Bears, okay. Snakes, iffy but doable. Crawling, multi-legged insects . . . no.

"Here's another gem. 'Don't bother showering if you stay here. You'll just get dirty again walking out of the room.' And my personal favorite, 'This dump needs gasoline and a match.'" He couldn't help his chuckle. Then the reality of the reviews hit him. "*Does* it need to be torn down?"

"No." She hesitated, and Jake wondered what she'd gotten into. "Well, at least I don't think it does. Joey went by and looked at the foundation, roof, and the rest of the exterior. It all needed improvement but appeared solid."

Her contractor on-again-off-again boyfriend knew his business. "Maybe it's just a bad housekeeping team?"

"Exactly. Someone isn't doing their job. Clean it up. Slap some paint on it along with a new roof. Turn a profit." She talked faster and faster. That usually meant she wanted him to do something.

"Pull on your rubber gloves and get out your scrub brush. You're losing money every day it's a dump."

The phone crackled, but she didn't say anything. Lizzie and silence didn't go together.

"Where are you, sis?"

"Bali."

He laughed. "Seriously. Where are you?"

"Bali. I'm on an island. A client wanted me to redecorate his family's vacation home. I've committed to being here for the next month."

"You can't fly home for the weekend, right?"

Lizzie made a sound between a laugh and a groan. "I spent a day on the plane getting here. So that's a no." She sighed yet again. "Jake—"

"Please don't say it."

"You're my only choice."

"What about Joey? A contractor would be great for this."
He hoped.

"One of my friends took a phone photo of him and a well-endowed blonde mid-seduction in a restaurant yesterday."

"I'll send Leo."

"Jake, a construction manager isn't the same as my brother."

Pushing back his exhaustion, he said, "Text me the address." He turned the key in the ignition. "I'll let you know what I find."

"You're the best."

Seconds later, his phone signaled a text.

"I'm into it for a chunk of change right now," she said. "Do what you have to and as cheaply as possible so I can sell it."

He checked the address she'd sent. "I'm on my way."

Jake groaned when he saw the motel. The glory days of Lizzie's new property were long gone. It looked like something from an old movie, maybe one of the creepier movies by Alfred Hitchcock.

He walked the perimeter. As Joey had said, the structure appeared sound. Entering the lobby, he found it empty with no one at the front desk—only the stench of a cheap cigar hung in the air. The cleaning staff lounged in a room to the side. After firing them, he grabbed a couple of keys for rooms that the old-fashioned register book—seriously?— showed were empty.

When he opened the first door, Lizzie's crisis escalated.

This might have to be stripped to the wall studs. The second room mirrored the first.

Returning to the lobby, he found a man behind the front desk with a mess of papers and bills stacked on top. Well, stacked would be an exaggeration. It would be better described as a random mess. Only the room bills were in order.

Jake set down the keys.

"Who are you?" the man asked around a cigar.

"I'm the new owner's representative."

"Huh." He stared at Jake as though waiting for him to further explain himself.

"You are?"

"Herb Reynolds," he said, followed by a wheeze.

"Do you work here every day, Herb?"

Herb shrugged. "Most days. We're busy here." He patted the papers on his desk.

Jake stared at him. The papers in that pile didn't look as though they had been moved recently.

"I need to, uh, check something." The man moved around Jake as though he knew he wanted to fire him on the spot. Instead, Jake would wait to decide his fate.

A noise caused him to turn. A woman wearing sunglasses and with her hair tucked up into a ball cap stepped out of the door next to him with a stack of sheets and towels in her arms.

She stopped. "I found the door open, and no one here, so I got my own clean linens." She lifted the stack in her arms. "Now that I've finished cleaning the room, I thought fresh sheets would be a good idea."

His eyebrows shot upward. "Finished, as in it's clean now?"

15

She shrugged. "Honestly, I wasn't going to sleep in it as it was. I didn't even want to wash my hands in that sink let alone brush my teeth. And that shower?" She shuddered. "Not happening."

Maybe his sister's hotel could be saved for a reasonable amount of money.

"I'd like to see what it looks like clean. Would you mind if I checked your room?"

She seemed to hesitate.

"I promise I'll stand in the doorway if you're concerned."

She laughed. "No. That's not it. You seem like a decent guy, and I'm usually a good judge of people. But I'm not a professional cleaner. I may not be very good at it."

He started for the door. "I'm not going to judge you. I truly want to see what's going on underneath all the filth. My sister just bought this motel, and I'm helping her out while she's out of the country." He started for the door.

She followed behind him as they left the lobby and went back outside to the sidewalk that ran the length of the building. Then he paused, and she rammed into his back.

He turned around and reached for her arm to steady her. "Sorry! I don't know what room you're in, and even if I did, I couldn't tell you where it was in this building." She pointed around him, and he waved her on, following her. He really wasn't going to complain about the view of her in snug jeans, which probably made him a typical guy.

She stepped up to room Forty's door, inserted the key, then moved aside.

He opened the door and a fresh scent wafted out. The dresser was grime-free, and the vinyl-covered chair that had been a dark-something color in the rooms he'd seen was light blue. His gaze moved down to the floor, which appeared to be clean. "Did you shampoo the carpet?"

"I hope you don't mind. I found the carpet cleaner in the storage room along with the fluid and directions, so I went ahead and did the carpet. I think it'll be damp all night. But I didn't want to walk on that floor either."

"Mind?" He laughed. "You have transformed this into a place I wouldn't mind staying in. And I have to tell you that I'm relieved for my sister."

"I think if you just add some new bed covers and maybe painted an accent wall behind the bed, this place would be very appealing to those who don't want to stay in a large hotel. A lot of music people would be interested in it because it's less expensive too."

He could see her vision. "Have you worked in the music industry?"

After a few seconds' pause, she said, "I've done just about everything in the music industry at one time or another."

"Nashville *is* Music City, USA, so that isn't a surprise. Even my painting contractor dreams of singing at the Grand Ole Opry."

She laughed, and he liked the sound of it.

Before he walked farther into her room, he asked, "Would you mind if I checked out the bathroom?"

"Of course not."

He noticed, though, that she stayed by the door instead of following him into the room, and that was probably a good safety precaution she'd picked up somewhere in her life. The bathroom had been scrubbed with the same attention to detail. Now he could tell that the tub enclosure with white tiles had been redone at some point; he guessed about a decade earlier judging from the style and the condition. After fresh paint inside and out, along with a new roof, this would be a place his sister could be proud of and sell.

He went back into the room and through it to stand outside so they could have a conversation she'd be comfortable with. He rarely hired someone without running a background check, but she worked hard, and he needed someone immediately. "You wouldn't by any chance want a job, would you?"

CHAPTER THREE

*C*harlotte stared at him. There was every possibility that this handsome man was offering her a job as this motel's housekeeper. She respected people in all kinds of work and always made a point of treating everyone equally, but it was a big jump from singing and songwriting to cleaning forty-plus hours a week. And this wasn't just changing sheets and dusting. This would be scrubbing away years of grime to bring a filthy building back to life.

Her bank balance flashed into her mind. If she took the job, she'd have a paycheck in probably a couple of weeks. If she didn't, it could be weeks before she had any other offer, and then she'd have to wait for a first paycheck. What would she do then?

This was crazy, but it wouldn't be the first crazy thing she'd done. "If you're offering a job at this motel, I'll take it. Mr.—?" She extended her hand to shake his.

"Anderson. Jake Anderson. Call me Jake." His introduction sounded as formal as his dress shirt and trousers that probably paired with a suit coat. His only hint of rugged rebellion: his almost-beard and mustache in the same dark blond as his perfectly trimmed hair.

"Charlotte McDaniel." She extended her hand to him.

When he took her hand, warmth oozed through her, then a zing tingled her insides. She struggled to focus on him as he spoke.

"Yes, I am offering you a job as a housekeeper, lead housekeeper, here at the Bates Motel."

"Excuse me? The Bates Motel?"

He rolled his eyes. "I'm sorry. The more time I spend here trying to figure out this mess my sister left me in, the more I've come to think of it as the Bates Motel. You know, like the Alfred Hitchcock movie with the serial killer."

She shuddered. "That's a creepy movie. Now you've put that image in my mind."

He glanced at the sign and back to her. "I do think we'll have to rename the motel, because the nasty reviews tied to the current name would follow my sister forever."

She grinned. "Probably not that name, though. Maybe something musical-sounding."

"Good plan. Nashville has all kinds of music, but visitors often think it's all country. Maybe a name that goes with music." He seemed to think about it. "Nothing comes to mind, probably because I'm actually a jazz fan. How about you?"

"Country music and bluegrass all the way. Although I don't mind a little jazz now and then."

He glanced at his watch. "It's late. I put in a long work week, and you spent hours cleaning this soon-to-be-former dump. Why don't we get started again tomorrow morning? If you don't mind working on the weekend."

She'd work at midnight if it got her a paycheck faster.

"Sounds like a good plan. It has been a very long day." Just saying those words reminded her of where she'd started the day. From her mansion to here.

"It will be Saturday, so I can be here all day. Let's meet at eight at the front desk."

Charlotte agreed and gave a small wave as she closed and locked the door. She watched his shadow pass by her front window, then danced around the room. "I have a job!"

She stopped and surveyed her new home. She could begin a new life here. Loud voices in the parking lot made her glad she'd locked the door. Pulling off her ball cap, she said, "Carly has to disappear." She picked up the box of hair color and went into the bathroom to become a brunette.

Charlotte opened her eyes when her phone alarm played "Dueling Banjos," a song that always forced her to wake up. Handsome Jake Anderson had featured in her dreams. She'd scrubbed, and he'd been about to kiss her out of gratitude. Then she'd heard the music.

Stretching, she debated taking a shower, but concluded that bathing before immersing yourself in filth didn't make sense. Last night's shower had relaxed tight muscles, and she'd need that again tonight. At least the bed was decent. Not too hard, not too soft.

Spending time with Jake wouldn't be a trial. He didn't wear a wedding ring, but you couldn't always tell a man's marital status by the absence of a ring. He probably had a sweet, beautiful wife at home and three adoring children. He knew nothing about country music, it seemed, so her identity was safe here. Just as she'd hoped.

She got out of bed and went into the bathroom where a slightly different woman was reflected in the mirror. She fingered her newly brown, wavy hair, which reached her waist without her usual tighter curls. She'd been too tired to do any more than color it last night, but she had told Maggie she'd cut it. A quick snip with the scissors she'd bought yesterday trimmed off an inch.

The face in the mirror had barely changed. She held open scissors a few inches below her left shoulder, closed her eyes and snipped. Opening first one eye and then the other, she found a new woman. This woman would have a fresh start. After matching the length all around, she added light makeup. Charlotte did look different from Carly. She gave a satisfied nod.

She brushed her hair, then her teeth, grateful for her clean oasis in this motel. Then she dressed in her oldest jeans and a T-shirt a fan had given her that said, "Sunshine is the best medicine."

When she went downstairs, she found Jake in the lobby rifling through papers on the desk again, this time while talking on the phone.

"Lizzie, this place is a mess. I've hired a new housekeeper—"

Was Lizzie his wife? Girlfriend?

He raised his eyes upward as he paused, and she must have kept speaking.

"Yes, there *was* a housekeeper. Actually, there *were* three members of the housekeeping staff. When I walked in yesterday, I found them sitting in the supply room with a beer in one hand, a cigarette in the other, and their feet up on five-gallon containers of cleaning liquids." He held his phone away from his ear. "No, I didn't get carried away with myself. This place is a dump. The rooms are even more filthy than the reviews said, if that's possible." Then there was another pause. "No, I'm not being a neat freak." He glanced Charlotte's way. "The manager is questionable too. I have to go now, Lizzie. I hope to know the status of your purchase soon. My new housekeeper just arrived. I'm going to spend the day cleaning with her."

Charlotte felt the breath whoosh out of her. He would clean *with* her? This gorgeous man who had given her wakeful moments in the night was going to be in a small motel room with her for the entire day? *Ignore him, Charlotte. A romance would not be the best way to start your new life.*

He looked up at her again and gave a small wave. "No, I'm not sleeping with the help. She's the housekeeper, Lizzie."

Cold water washed over her. He would not have a relationship with the housekeeper. A year ago, she'd been the one everyone wanted to date. It amazed her how social class in America determined your love life.

He glanced up at her. "I'll be there in just a moment, Charlotte."

To the phone, he said, "I know. I know. I will take care of it. I promise. You'll be able to sell this motel soon. It's going to take some cash, and you'll owe me out of the sale price." There was another pause. Then he ended the call by saying, "Yes. I may be the best brother in the entire world. Bye, sis. Love you."

A warm and fuzzy feeling went through Charlotte's body. Not a girlfriend or wife. And he was nice to his sister. This was probably a man who liked kittens and babies, two of her favorite things on earth. Her "no romance now" concept would be easy to uphold when she was his housekeeper, though. He'd made his feelings about her clear.

Mister Button-Down stepped around the counter, but today he was wearing jeans and a shirt that hugged an upper body that must have spent hours in a gym. Whew!

"Let's get going, Charlotte. We'll see how far we can get today. I know I need to hire more staff, but I haven't had time to do that yet. Today should tell us how many people it will take to get my sister's motel into a state where she can sell it and not lose money."

Charlotte's shoulder brushed his upper arm as she went past him in the narrow corridor leading to the utility closet. Tingles ran from shoulder to fingertips. Definitely attraction there on her part. *Don't fall for the boss, Charlotte.*

When Jake's phone rang, he stayed in place in the corridor and had a business conversation while she stacked the things they'd need onto a rolling cart. She pushed it out into the lobby, then went back and got the carpet cleaner and cleaning solution. They had enough to do maybe five rooms before they had to order more. But she was going to need a day off after cleaning that many rooms, anyway. A housekeeping workout was more intense than any gym.

They began with the guest room closest to the office, neither of them speaking as they cleaned the bathroom. The silence grew harder and harder to take. Should she interrupt the quiet when her boss seemed to want that? Just when she wasn't sure she could take another thirty seconds of it, Jake spoke up.

"This task is right up there with the time my grandmother got mad at her grandsons and had us scrub her bathroom floor with toothbrushes." He sat back on his heels and wiped his brow with his sleeve. "I remember hating every second of that day."

"But it did make you appreciate a clean bathroom, didn't it?"

He laughed. "It did at that. To make our day more interesting, Charlotte, tell me about yourself. I didn't run a background check on you, so I don't know anything about you."

Charlotte was grateful he couldn't see her face right now. She turned on the tub's spigot and rinsed the tiles in the surround. As she turned off the water, she wondered what she could say.

"I was born in California? Is that the kind of thing you want to know?"

"I want you to entertain me with fascinating stories of your life. *Please* help this day go faster. You can make things up if you want to. Keep it interesting, though, if you go that direction. And let me guess if it's real or not."

She sat on the edge of the bathtub and faced him. "I'm warning you. I have a vivid imagination."

"Give it your best shot."

She had a decade of performing to draw on. "Okay, I'll tell you about the time I met the Queen of England."

Laughing, he threw the sponge in the sink and turned toward her. "It turns out that I do have rules after all. That's too far-fetched."

Charlotte chuckled. She had actually met the Queen of England, and it made a fun tale. But she'd go with something a little closer to home.

"You didn't buy my meeting the Queen, so let's see. How about my singing on stage at the Grand Ole Opry? That'll make a great story."

Jake grinned, and oh what a grin it was. "Sounds like you'll be telling a whopper, but go for it."

Charlotte thought about her many performances at the Opry and chose her best story. "This is about one time when the Opry was at the Ryman Auditorium. I always dreamed of performing in such a historic venue, right in downtown Nashville. My custom-made costume was covered in sequins, and if I remember correctly, and I believe I do, they were white with an iridescent pink pearl. The light caught them with every move I made." She ran her hands down the sides of her body, his eyes following. Interesting.

"My drummer broke his wrist, and we found a last-minute replacement—Steve, who lived in a small town an hour away. He dragged in seconds before the show with a stranger who had rescued him from the side of a country road after his car broke down. We gave the Good Samaritan a seat in the wings as a thank you."

"Nice details."

"Thank you, sir." Charlotte bowed. Then she picked up her spray bottle of cleaner and paper towels. "This bathroom is clean."

"Good job. Before seeing your room, I wouldn't have thought that possible without a full remodel."

Feeling good about a job well done, Charlotte headed out the bathroom door. She had learned how to clean. She was an overcomer. She would find a way out of this no-money, no-music-career situation.

Jake followed Charlotte out of the bathroom. The new housekeeper was quite a spitfire with an amazing imagination. He was finding himself having a little too much fun with her. He may have been dubbed one of Nashville's most eligible men, but he never dallied—did anyone still use the word *dallied?*—with anyone who might see him as her gravy train. It sounded cold and harsh, but he only dated women who had as much money as he did. Then he knew they wanted him for himself.

And he always, without exception, kept a business-only relationship with employees.

If his sister were here, she'd ask, "How's all that working for you, Jake?" The honest answer was, not very well.

He checked his watch and realized they'd worked longer than he'd expected. "Do you want lunch?"

She stood. "Sure. Let me grab something from my room."

He put his hand on her arm, then pulled it back. "I meant that we could go get lunch."

Gesturing at herself, she said, "I don't think I'm dressed for going out."

"I'll run and get us something. A sandwich okay with you."

"Anything is fine."

He left, found a sandwich chain shop, and returned with a selection of sandwiches. Standing in the doorway, he watched Charlotte cleaning the chair, scrubbing it to within an inch of its life. "Ready?"

She jumped. "Don't scare me like that." She glanced at the bag in his hands. "Good choice. I like their food."

They sat down, him on the edge of the bed, her on the chair she'd been cleaning, and ate quietly, but, this time, it was a pleasant quiet.

She crunched up the paper her sandwich had been wrapped in. "Thank you! I feel better now."

He took the last bite of his own meal. "Are you ready for my story?"

She turned to face him, pushing a strand of hair off her forehead with the back of her hand. "Bring it on! And you never told me if you thought my story was true or false."

He laughed. "You spin a great tale, but it's false. Maybe you should consider writing a novel."

She smiled the same way she had last night, one best described as a secret smile. Like she knew something he didn't. And that was probably true. He was a man, and men often seemed to miss the obvious. At least his mother and sister kept telling him that.

Jake began a story about "one of the times" he'd had lunch with the president of the United States. How likely was it that their country's leader ate lunch with someone like either of them?

Charlotte laughed when he described the extravagant dessert. "And you accused *me* of having a vivid imagination."

"So you vote false story? Is that correct?"

She nodded. "You bet I do." She turned the chair around and sprayed the back of it. "The next thing you'll tell me is that you have a sports car sitting in the parking lot. A black one. Something foreign and expensive."

Silence greeted her, so she turned toward him. He wore a stunned expression.

"What?" Had she stepped over the line between boss and employee? They'd been acting like friends.

He walked away, and she thought, this is it, the end of the good times. He opened the door and said, "Charlotte, I want you to see my wheels."

She followed him to the parking lot. He pointed out a

low-slung black sports car of a make and model she could not discern, probably foreign. When she got closer, she read, "Lamborghini."

Wheeling around, she looked at him, then took a step back. "You're rich? What are you doing here?"

"You know I'm helping my sister. I've done well flipping properties of my own, and that car was one of my treats to myself."

Charlotte went over to it and leaned down to look inside. "Have you had her long? She's a beauty."

He lovingly touched the hood. "A few months."

She suspected that this car cost more than the average house. Housekeepers and wealthy men didn't date, so that ended any hope for a date with Jake Anderson. She stood and straightened her shoulders. "Let's get this finished, Jake."

"I'll be there in just a minute. I have to make a quick phone call." His took his phone out of his back pocket.

She raised an eyebrow.

"Don't worry. I *will* be there. I'm not trying to put off working. It isn't my favorite kind of work, but she is my favorite sister."

"How many sisters do you have?"

"One."

Charlotte laughed and started back. If she'd had a brother, she would have wanted one like him.

Jake stood next to his car and hit speed dial. As he waited for the call to be answered, he looked around and up, again evaluating the motel's needs.

His mother answered.

"Mom, what are you and Dad doing today?"

When he'd shared the wonders of Nashville with his family, both his sister and his parents had moved here. He sincerely hoped they didn't have any plans for this week. He could use a couple more able-bodied and free hands on board. Lizzie would want to pay for anyone he hired, and he knew she wanted to keep costs down. Besides, they would act like a buffer between himself and Charlotte. The new housekeeper intrigued him more than she should.

"We're in Boston on business," his mother replied, "but we're returning a couple of days after Mom arrives in Nashville."

The motel had made him forget that his grandmother would be coming for a visit in a few days, and she'd be staying at his house. His parents had downsized a couple of years ago to a two-story, two-bedroom condo, and the bedrooms were upstairs. He'd built his house with an elevator for times such as this.

"I wasn't thinking of Mom when we bought our new place, but thank you for letting her stay with you."

"Are you kidding? I love having Grandma here."

"You live like a bachelor. Get someone to clean her bedroom and bathroom!"

He managed, "Yes, ma'am," before he heard her say, "A meeting's about to start. Bye." The call ended.

The roofline caught his eye. The shingles had to be replaced, and soon, but few guests would want to stay there with banging overhead all day for days. The most efficient plan would be to shut everything down, get the roof done, and bring in a cleaning team. As they'd found today, going room by room would take a long time. Maybe as much as a month, and they'd still need to paint and replace carpeting. Lizzie needed this on the market as soon as possible.

Plan complete, he scrolled through his phone and called the roofer he used on his projects, setting up a time later that day for him to come out and give an estimate.

Now, he just needed to print out a sign to hang on all the doors to tell residents what would be happening next week. They'd have time to find a new place. He may have to give a refund to some guests who had paid in advance, but he didn't see any other choice.

Charlotte and her smile came to mind. He'd just given her a job. The woman had taken it because she needed one, but now he'd be snatching it right back.

A text message came in from his personal chef, Marta.

Your mother called to ask me to clean her mother's room. I must remind you that I do not clean anything but the kitchen. Please find a new cleaner or chef.

Marta happily accommodated food requests for visitors, so his mother had her phone number. His chef cooked amazing food and planned meals to suit his often work-caused inconsistent meal times. The problem was that his twice-a-week cleaning woman had quit a few weeks ago. She had been slacking off on cleanliness, so he hadn't been disappointed, but he had been too busy to replace her.

Grandma would be there for two weeks, more or less. The house would have to be cleaned before and during her stay. He'd ask a cleaning company to send someone to his house every day.

As he walked back into the almost-clean room, a way to solve two problems came to mind. "Charlotte, I have a great idea."

She looked up from the dresser she'd been wiping down, waiting for him to speak.

"I'm going to have a team of cleaners come in and take care of this job."

Her face fell.

He knew then that she truly needed this job. She was a hard worker, and she liked things clean, just as his grandmother did. "I have a new idea, if you're interested. My grandmother is coming for a visit, and my house is in what my mother not-so-lovingly calls 'bachelor condition.' I had a woman who cleaned twice a week, but she recently quit."

She raised an eyebrow. "Not grandmother-ready?"

"It isn't filthy. Nothing like this motel." He gestured around him. "But you can't eat off the floor. Not that anyone really wants to," he muttered.

Charlotte leaned against the dresser.

"Well, I've paid for a month here. Do you live nearby? I can go back and forth every day if that's okay with you."

"Unfortunately, no. I just realized that I hadn't mentioned my plan to close the motel while the roof is being replaced."

Now she gripped the dresser as though it could support her.

He'd taken her job *and* her home. He lived about twenty minutes away, but his house had a room off the kitchen for a housekeeper along with a private bath. His cook lived off-site and only worked five days a week. He'd never had live-in staff, had never wanted that constant intrusion into his privacy, but he could do it short term for his grandmother. Would Charlotte like that idea? That was the question.

"I have a suite in my home that was designed for live-in help. I've occasionally had a friend bunk there when they were passing through town because it's private and set away from the part of the house where I spend most of my time." She seemed to be sizing him up, so he added, "My grandmother will be there soon, so you'll have a chaperone. And she's very conservative in her ideas about unmarried men and women."

She only hesitated for a few seconds. "I'll take the job."

"Excellent. Why don't you stay here tonight? Let's stop cleaning now that we know the plan. Someone else will finish. I'll give you my address, and you can move in Sunday afternoon. You can back out if you decide to. No pressure. But if you like it, then I'll just let you continue working there as long as Grandma stays."

"You're trusting a woman you just met?"

He shrugged. "I'm usually a good judge of character. You clean amazingly well with such attention to detail. And if you wanted to take anything, you could have robbed the motel blind, shoved your room's collector's item of a vinyl-covered chair in your vehicle and just hightailed it out of here."

She laughed. "Who knows what value that could have? Okay, I'll see you tomorrow afternoon."

They exchanged numbers, and he sent her a text that included a gate code.

As soon as he left, she sent Maggie a text. *Got a job!*

Her friend replied, *Great! Doing?*

She suspected that Maggie would be on the next plane if she knew the whole story.

I'll tell you more when I see if it works out.

33

CHAPTER FOUR

*C*harlotte's life had changed so much. From country music star to rich man's housekeeper. At least it should pay decently. It had to pay more than the jobs she'd expected to apply for starting today. Her resume was woefully short and lacking in traditional skills. But she still should have asked about that.

Maybe Jake would decide he needed her even after his grandmother went home. In six months, she could have enough money to record a new demo—if she was really careful with every penny she got. Forgetting about her attraction to her boss would also help her have a better future.

She grabbed the pile of paper towels she and Jake had used and stuffed them into a trash bag. She picked up the scrub brush and realized she'd worn it out. After throwing that in the bag too, she carried the bag out and around to the rear of the building where she assumed she'd find a dumpster.

Then she carried their leftover cleaning supplies to the

office and let herself inside using the key Jake had given her, expecting to find it empty. Instead, she heard a guitar being strummed with a male voice singing along to a song she recognized, one she'd actually sung quite a few times. Not a hit, but an old standard that was a fan favorite.

Moving inside, she saw a man in his early twenties wearing the musician's uniform of slightly shaggy hair—his dark brown—a T-shirt, and as she got closer, she could see jeans. You could go anywhere in Nashville wearing that, including the symphony, but you'd probably want to put on one of your nicer T-shirts and pairs of jeans.

It seemed unlikely that a vagrant musician would break into a motel's front office late at night and play music. Although with what she'd heard some bands were paying their musicians, he might simply need a roof over his head.

She said, "I'm supposed to be here. . ."

The music stopped, and he looked up from the guitar. "Mitch Bailey at your service." He winced. "That was a bit cliché, wasn't it?"

She laughed. "I can live with it. What are you doing here, Mitch?"

"I'm the night manager. Which leads me to ask, what are *you* doing here? I know everyone who has a key, and you aren't one of those people." He set his guitar to the side.

"I was hired as the housekeeper today."

"Pleased to meet you. George didn't mention that he was hiring anyone new." He stood and reached across the front desk to shake her hand.

Charlotte set the cleaner down and shook his hand. "Who's George?"

"*George.* The owner of this fine establishment." He patted the check-in counter.

"Oh, the former owner. I think I met him yesterday."

He cocked his head sideways. "Okaay. And what happened to Sylvia, Joyce, and Carmen?"

"Unfortunately, if those names you just mentioned were in housekeeping, all three were fired yesterday because they were smoking and drinking instead of cleaning."

Mitch groaned and rubbed his hand over his face. "I told them that might happen. Anyway, I knew this place was for sale, but George told me I would be one of the first to know if he even had an offer. And it sold? Who to?" He scuffed his shoe on the floor. "Scratch that. My bigger question is, what am I going to do now? Working here every night I didn't have a gig is what's been putting a roof over my head and food in my belly." He pointed to his stomach for emphasis.

Charlotte understood exactly what he was going through. She'd started out that way; most musicians here in Nashville did, wondering when they'd get their next gig and with it their next paycheck. Sure she'd found success, major success, but his story was one that was repeated over and over again around Nashville every day of every year. And now here she was with him in this dive of a motel.

"A woman bought the inn. Lizzie. I'm not sure about her last name, but it's probably Anderson. Her brother is getting it in shape because she wants to sell it to make a profit. A lot of work needs to be done, including cleaning."

"I guess you're on the level."

"Because I don't look like a vagrant?"

"No, because I've seen those three ladies knock back a few brews when they should be working. And this place is a pigsty. I keep my room in decent shape, at least for a guy." He grinned.

Charlotte laughed. "Mine wasn't. I came in here to get

stuff to clean with and did a good enough job that I was hired as the housekeeper."

He stared at her, not in a way that said he was interested in her as a woman, but curious. "Something about you doesn't say starving artist. You look familiar."

She flushed. Would he know who she was?

"You in music?"

Since he hadn't called her out by name, she figured she was safe. "I've played a bit."

He laughed. "That could mean anything in this town."

Mitch strummed his guitar and sang a few more lines of the song.

"Tell me about your career? Any decent gigs yet?"

Charlotte put the bottles and rolls of paper towels on a shelf, then stepped back out and listened as he played. "Give it a bit more on the second phrase."

He stopped and stared at her. "You *are* a musician, aren't you?"

She shrugged. "It's Nashville."

He laughed. Then he sang the song and did as she'd said. At the end, he tilted his head to the side and gave her a steady gaze. "That made the song better. Any other tips?"

She realized she didn't have to hide knowing about music. Only her real identity. "Play it like you mean it."

He grinned and dove into the song. When he finished, he put his hands over the strings to quiet them and gave her the same look.

"Let's see what we can do. When you got to the beginning of the chorus, you hesitated. Try that softly, more heartfelt, and without hesitation."

He played the section again. Right after that, he leaned

back in his chair with a startled expression on his face. "That's *much* better. Degree in music?"

She shook her head. "No. But I have spent a lot of time with a guitar in my hands. What about you? Did you go to school for music?"

"Nope. My parents didn't want to pay for," he held up his hands for air quotes, "a worthless degree that wouldn't bring in a paycheck." Dropping his hands, he added, "Nothing in the arts suited them, so I chose a degree that allowed me to work outside: landscape architect. I thought if I couldn't make it in music, at least I wouldn't have to sit behind a desk somewhere. But here I am." He grinned.

Her last conversation with Jake came to mind. "Mitch, they're going to ask everyone to move out. A new roof's going on ASAP, and there will be hammering all day."

He closed his eyes and sighed. "That would eliminate sleeping during the day, wouldn't it?" He opened his eyes and stared at her with a weary expression, one far beyond his years.

"Maybe you could find a job doing landscape work on your days off."

"At night?"

"When do you get out of bed the morning after a gig?"

"About two in the afternoon."

"Good to know. Your words made me think you were a vampire. What if you worked between when you got up and dark?"

"But where will I live?"

"I'll give this some thought and get back to you." She moved toward the door.

"Thanks! Hey, what's your name?"

"Charlotte."

"Great. I'll call you Charlie."

She froze. Too close to Carly. She took a deep breath and looked over her shoulder. "I think we'd better stick with Charlotte."

He grinned and shrugged. "It just seemed like you needed a music name, and Charlotte doesn't sound like one to me."

"You're right about that." She opened the door and went outside. If only she could be interested in someone like Mitch—someone accessible, someone she could actually have a relationship with—but no, she had to be attracted to a wealthy man who must live in a large home.

Wondering about her own new home reminded Charlotte of her current residence and the disaster of landscaping around it. That gave her an idea.

She grabbed her phone and sent a text to Jake, telling him he had a night manager named Mitch who seemed to be doing a good job and hadn't known about the change in ownership. She added, *He's trained as a landscape architect. Would you consider him for the landscaping around this building? Oh, and he'll need a place to live when they're doing the roof because he's also a musician who plays at night, so he sleeps during the day.*

She dropped the phone on the bed.

Her phone dinged. *I have landscape architects that I routinely use in my business.*

Charlotte felt her heart sink. He'd been her one solution to Mitch's problem.

He continued. *But considering the fact that this man has done his best and was probably the reason that the room billing was up to date, I'm going to hire him to do this. He's been living at that inn, so he probably deserves a break.*

Another text arrived. *There's a small room and bathroom*

beside the pool at my house. Tell him he can stay there while the roof is being worked on and give him the gate code.

Seconds later, he followed with, *After that, we'll have to paint and do some other work at the motel, so he can live there as long as it takes to get the inn back to a livable state.*

She replied, *I will let him know.*

Charlotte hurried out the door, carefully locking it, then looking around before she stepped away to make sure there weren't any shady characters hanging around. She definitely had some good defenses built up after years of being on tour. But she did have to say that there had never been a motel as shady as this one.

When she unlocked and entered the front office, Mitch glanced up. "Need more cleaning supplies?"

She went over and leaned on the check-in counter. "I have great news for you." She explained what Jake had said.

As she spoke, Mitch's blue eyes opened wider and wider. When she got to the part about him staying there as long as it took to get the inn in good shape, he stood, and said, "Are you kidding?"

She shook her head.

"This is the best thing that's happened since I moved to Nashville. I can play music at night. Sleep. *And* do landscape work. Plus I get to live next to the pool at some rich guy's house?"

"That about sums it up. I've been pretty happy about how my life has gone today too."

He picked up his guitar and started strumming. Charlotte recognized the tune but not the words he sang to it. This time his voice held more hope.

CHAPTER FIVE

*A*fter church, Charlotte drove to Jake's address. She pulled to the curb in front of a mailbox with the numbers Jake had texted. A mansion, a modern castle really, with clean lines and angles, set back from the road on a hill. It must be twice the size of her old house. Either he had made a mistake with the address, or he had a whole lot more money than she'd realized.

Of course, when a man had a pool house, that did lead one to believe he had a lot of cash. Although he did say a small room with a bathroom.

She eased the truck forward and stared at the long gated driveway, hoping to see his car. But of course, it would be parked in a stall in a five- or ten-car garage off to the side. Or he was at work.

Charlotte pulled up to the gate. Shrugging, she said, "I guess I'm going in. Either this is the right place, or it isn't." She entered the code, and the gate started to swing open.

At the top of the long driveway, she pulled up by a side door, assuming the help did not go to the front entrance. A petite woman wearing chef's whites with the name Marta embroidered on the coat answered the door. If Tinker Bell had a side hustle as a chef, this would be her.

"Can I help you with something?" the woman asked. "I don't mean to be rude, but I need to hurry because I have a sauce on the stove, and I can't walk away from it for more than a minute." She glanced back over her shoulder.

"Is this the home of Jake Anderson?" Charlotte said.

The pixie sighed. "I don't know how you got the gate code, but I don't think you're his type, honey." She started to push the door shut.

"I'm his new housekeeper."

The woman lunged at her and hugged her tightly. "Thank goodness! His grandmother is coming for a visit, and his mother expected me to clean the house *and* make food for the family." She pulled the door back and waved Charlotte inside. "Come in. Come in." She raced over to the stove and began whisking something in a pan. "I'll gladly share whatever I know about the house and your job."

Charlotte closed the door and stood in a kitchen every bit as grand as the one in her old house. The somewhat stark white cupboards and tile backsplash with gray and white granite counters were softened by wood beams overhead.

One major difference between this kitchen and her old one was that hers had been part of an open great room, but this one had a swinging door that sealed it off from the rest of the house. Probably because Jake would only have others cooking for him.

"Sit at one of the stools at the island and ask as many questions as you like," Marta said. "I'm Marta Martino."

Charlotte did as instructed, pulling out the metal and wood chair, a combination of the two textures that she appreciated, and sat at the huge island. "I'm Charlotte McDaniel. Is he messy? I've gotten the impression that he's very neat and tidy."

Marta laughed. "He's a fussy bachelor. He briefly dated a woman with a dog. . . I guess that was about a year ago, and he didn't like it coming into the house because of the muddy footprints."

Charlotte put her elbow on the granite island and leaned her fist into the side of her mouth. At least this was a best-case scenario for her to get information about Jake. Marta was a woman who was so thrilled that help had arrived that she'd spill about her employer when she might not otherwise. Although she might just be chatty all the time.

"Does he use the whole house, or will I only be cleaning a few rooms? Or do you know that?"

Marta lifted the sauce off of the burner and set it in a bowl of ice. Then she began washing strawberries.

"Mr. Anderson will have to tell you what he wants, but from what I've seen, he uses most of the main living areas, but only his bedroom out of the six. When he has guests, then, of course, there's more to do. Each bedroom has its own bathroom. He built the house to suit his needs, but also for guests."

Marta cut off the tops of the strawberries and started slicing them.

"So he doesn't have any children?"

She shook her head. "No, and he doesn't have a girlfriend right now either, if you're wondering that." She turned and gave Charlotte a grin.

Charlotte laughed. "He is easy on the eyes, isn't he?"

Marta returned to her slicing. "Tall and handsome? He is that. When I started working for him a couple of years ago, there was a little piece of me that wouldn't have minded a fling with the boss, but he has a clear separation between his personal and private life. I don't think he would ever have a relationship with someone who worked for him, at least not an employee. I know he briefly dated his decorator."

He might have been willing to date a country music star, but she'd lost her claim to fame an album ago. Oh sure, there were still people who knew who she was—there'd be people like that for years—but in the last year or so everyone asked either what she'd done lately or if she'd sing "Sunshine Cowboy" one more time. The answer to the first question was nothing that hit the charts. And the answer to the second question was, sure, if you write me a check. She'd sing "Twinkle, Twinkle Little Star" right now if someone paid her. The TJ mess had killed her last album, and no producer would have her after that.

When Marta switched to washing peaches, Charlotte stood. "I'll bring in my things now and get settled before Jake comes home."

Marta gave her a glance that said she was curious. "It's interesting that you call him Jake. I've never heard an employee call him anything other than Mr. Anderson. It isn't that he's terribly formal, it's just that line between business and personal."

"That's how he introduced himself. And that's what I've called him every time we've spoken. I guess I'll leave it to him to let me know if I need to change." He'd seemed very informal when she met him.

"That does sound like a good idea. He's a millionaire, and approaching being a billionaire, so he's earned the right to be eccentric." She turned toward Charlotte. "Just don't tell him I said so."

"A *billionaire?*" Charlotte struggled to pull oxygen into her lungs. This situation became stranger and stranger.

Marta nodded as she turned back to work and began peeling a peach as though his stellar finances weren't anything unusual. "His business grew a lot last year."

Charlotte looked for something to focus on, something other than Jake, the almost-billionaire. She pointed at the pile of strawberries and the growing amount of sliced peaches. "That seems like a lot of fruit for one man."

Marta laughed. "It would be for one serving. He likes to have a fresh fruit smoothie every morning, and I don't come in until about ten. I have the best hours! Because of that, I prepare fruit in advance and freeze it, so he just grabs it out of the freezer and tosses it in a blender. These are fresh Georgia peaches, and there isn't anything better than a fresh Georgia peach in July." She tossed the sliced peach onto a cookie sheet.

"I'll get started dusting and vacuuming in the morning. Do you know where the cleaning supplies are? You must need them for the kitchen, so you're probably on it."

Marta pointed toward a door off the kitchen. "That leads to a hallway and the garage. The laundry room door is off that hallway. Check the cabinets in there. I'm not sure what you'll find, because it's been up to his housekeeper to take care of it, and she hasn't come very often."

Charlotte's brow furrowed. "Jake said she was coming twice a week. That isn't right?"

"I didn't see her twice a week or remnants of cleanliness. But that might just be me. Mr. Anderson is pretty particular, so I have to assume the man knows when something is or isn't clean."

"Thanks." Charlotte started to walk away.

"Oh, and you'll park your vehicle in the last garage stall. I'll go into the garage and open it for you. Mr. Anderson can give you the garage remote. And if your car leaks anything—remember that whole thing about him being neat—make sure you grab one of the absorbent pads on the shelf to put under it so it'll catch the mess. He does that for a classic car he owns."

Charlotte was glad she'd left her boxes—also known as her luggage—at the motel. Walking into this house carrying cardboard boxes filled with everything she owned would strip away the last bits of dignity she had left. Tonight, when Marta was gone and Jake asleep, she'd get her things and bring them inside.

But she would happily check out her new room. A queen-sized bed with a fluffy white comforter, a cozy-looking gray-patterned chair, and a rustic wood dresser and steel and wood end tables added up to a comfortable, contemporary room. Except for some dust, it was clean, and done in a peaceful combination of soft grays with white accents. Her walk-in closet would hold ten times what she currently owned. The gray and white marble counters and coordinating tile in the bathroom added to the luxury of her room.

She'd settle in and begin working first thing Monday morning.

Jake came in through the garage and went in the side door to the house, hanging his keys on a pegboard by the door in the hallway. Marta would have a delicious meal waiting for him, one of the perks of business success.

She served him at the dining room table, which overlooked his backyard and pool. As he ate roast chicken, his mother's recipe for scalloped potatoes, and sautéed zucchini, movement near the pool house had him get to his feet and start for the door. Then he remembered he now had a guest staying there. And a housekeeper living in his house. He hoped he hadn't made a mistake hiring a landscaper he had never met and a housekeeper he barely knew. Something about her made him accept what she said as truth.

When he finished, he picked up garage remotes for each of them. Then he went out the French doors to the backyard and over to meet his guest, lighting around the pool cutting through the darkness. Knocking on the door, he was surprised to find it opened by Charlotte with a somewhat younger man, maybe about Lizzie's age, standing behind her. For some reason, his housekeeper's presence there bothered him, and he didn't know why because he wasn't one of those people who said his employees couldn't have relationships.

Charlotte smiled. "Jake! I'm glad you're here! Mitch arrived and knocked on the back door. I brought him out here. You said it was a room and a bath by the pool. Is this right?"

Jake could see a backpack and a guitar. "This is it. Will it do for you? Mitch, is it?"

Mitch put his hand out to shake Jake's. "Mitch Bailey, sir. This is the nicest thing anyone has done for me maybe in forever. I've been getting by at the inn and working nights off as the front desk manager, but it's great to have a break someplace good." His eyes widened. "Not that I meant your motel was bad."

Jake grinned. "First, it isn't my motel. It belongs to my sister. I'm just helping her sort it all out because she bought it and left the country for work. Second, she bought a motel that has problems. Feel free to speak your mind around me."

He looked at Mitch and then at Charlotte, and said, "I expect everyone who works for me to be honest. If you think something isn't going to work, please let me know." He smiled. "And if it's going very well, you can feel free to tell me that too."

They all laughed, and Mitch said, "I'll remember that."

"You're both living here and my grandmother will be here, so I'd like to run background checks. It's easy to do and at no charge to you. I'll have my assistant Harriet call you tomorrow."

Charlotte had a panicky expression. "I've never had one. Uh, what do they ask? Do you get my life history?"

Did she have something to hide? "Nothing like that. I just want to know if you have a criminal record."

She smiled. "I'm clean."

"Me too, boss. Except I got a speeding ticket last year." Mitch looked sheepish. "I was running late to a gig. Of course, I ended up getting there even later."

Smiling, Charlotte stepped outside. "Marta had me park in the garage. That's Mitch's car over there." She pointed to the right.

"Both of you have a garage bay for your vehicles. I'm not used to having anyone living in my house, but even guests receive a garage remote if needed." He handed them the devices.

"We both appreciate this," Charlotte said as she tucked the remote into her jeans pocket.

"Let's talk about the landscaping, Mitch. I wondered if you'd be interested in working on my garden while the motel's roof is being redone. I completed the front before I moved in about a year ago, but the back still needs work."

"I'll leave you two alone." Charlotte gave a small wave as she went out the open door.

After settling the terms, Jake went into his screened-in porch off the living room to enjoy the evening air. Charlotte and Mitch didn't act like a couple, more like friends. It made him happy to help both of them through these jobs.

If he was just doing something good, why did it seem so unsettling to have Charlotte living here?

When everyone had gone to bed, Charlotte turned off her bedroom lamp so no light would shine under the door and anyone coming into the kitchen would assume she had gone to sleep. Then she quietly went out her door and into the garage. Once there, she realized that the garage door opening and closing might wake someone up.

The overhead lights reflected off of Jake's five vehicles, all high-end. Then she realized that this wasn't an ordinary garage. A billionaire's house would have the best quality soundproofing between a garage and the rest of the building. She climbed into her truck, pushed the remote and left.

The motel felt more abandoned tonight with fewer cars in the lot. People must have read the signs Jake had posted this morning and be moving out.

She swallowed hard as she surveyed the parking lot before popping open the truck's door. Alone at night. A parking lot. A mostly abandoned motel.

Nothing about this made sense. She should have brought everything over earlier today.

Vanity got you here, Carly.

She rushed from her vehicle to her room. A couple of minutes later, hurried to her truck with her arms stacked with boxes. The sound of glass breaking came from nearby. She dropped the boxes in the bed of the truck and raced back for the few remaining things. With her pink boots tucked under one arm, and a plastic bag with her cosmetics over the other arm, she locked the door, ran to her truck, and got out of there.

Now, she just had to sneak back in.

When the gate closed behind Charlotte's truck as she started up the drive, a light came on in the kitchen. Jake must be getting a snack. Had he heard her leaving?

Her noisy vehicle idled halfway down the driveway as she waited, hoping he wouldn't come outside to find the source of the noise. When the light turned off, she breathed a sigh of relief, but she waited a few minutes before pulling up and into her garage bay.

With boxes in her arms, Charlotte tiptoed up the hall. She slowly turned the doorknob and opened the door a crack. Peering into the kitchen, she found it dark and empty. She went around the corner to her room and deposited most of her worldly goods on the bed before returning to the truck for the rest.

Minutes later, Charlotte sat on the bed. Smiling, she wondered if she had a potential career as a burglar.

CHAPTER SIX

*a*fter a night of dreams, almost nightmares really, about the background check, each one waking her up, Charlotte looked forward to getting on with her first day of work.

Something that sounded like a blender brought her out of her room. She'd dressed in jeans and a T-shirt but found Jake making a smoothie while wearing a dark-gray business suit, crisp white shirt and conservative tie.

"One for you too?" he asked.

"Thank you. I like to eat healthy."

He opened the full-sized freezer next to the fridge and brought out a container. "I do too, but with notable exceptions. I also have a muffin with breakfast most days. Marta marked this 'cinnamon streusel topped.' Want one?"

"Are you kidding? Yes!"

He popped a plate with two muffins on it into the microwave. "She does her best to make them lighter on the sugar."

Charlotte found the drawers with silverware and napkins. A housekeeper would probably set a place at the dining room table for her boss. Going out the kitchen door, she found an elegant dining room and a sun-filled room with windows lining two walls and a smaller round table. She put his place setting there. Then she returned to the kitchen and made a place for herself at the island.

"What are you doing?"

She stared at him. "Getting ready to eat?"

"Bring your plate to the table. You can eat with me."

This might be her first housekeeping gig, but she didn't think this was the norm.

She followed Jake, and he did go into what she'd call the breakfast room. Once seated, he seemed to be pondering something as he ate his muffin. "I should give you some direction. My main concerns are for my grandmother. Areas I'd like cleaned every day are her bedroom, bath, and a room I've set up as a private sitting area in the room next door. Otherwise, clean each area as necessary. I'm sure you'll do great."

"I may need some things for cleaning. How should I buy them?"

He set down his smoothie, and she thought she'd upset him. "I should have told you that. There's an envelope with cash in it in the drawer nearest the kitchen's outside door. Buy whatever supplies you believe we need and put a receipt in there. I check it at the end of the month." He took a sip of his smoothie, and Charlotte did the same, not sure if she should say anything more or be quiet as she expected a housekeeper should.

After another bite of his muffin, he said, "Charlotte, you

may have to help me be a boss in my home. A few years ago, I earned a good income as an architect. Then I started to flip properties and learned all I could. As my skills grew, I began flipping large commercial properties, and my income skyrocketed. All that is to say I've never learned to be comfortable with live-in employees, and I honestly see you more as a guest. With a paycheck." He grinned.

She couldn't help but grin back. "I can live with that."

Once she'd finished her smoothie and muffin—which were delicious, so much better than the snack bars she'd been eating on the cheap—she went back into the kitchen carrying their plates and glasses. She guessed that was probably expected of her, and he didn't correct her when she left or returned.

Jake pushed back his chair and stood. "Thank you for your work so far, Charlotte." With a grin, he added, "I'm off to the office."

She'd never met a man—other than a fellow artist—who enjoyed his work that much.

"Call or text if you have any questions." After those words, he picked up the suit coat he'd draped over a chair and went out the door.

Now it was time for her to work. That didn't make her feel like grinning, but she *was* grateful.

Being on the other side of the paycheck changed the rules. She'd always respected what other people did for her, but she apparently hadn't paid as much attention to them as she should have. Her house had been clean. The bathroom always looked shiny and sparkly. Becoming a star in your teens meant you didn't have to clean a whole lot of toilets.

She went down the hall that led to the garage. She tried

one door and found it opened to the main living area. That must be how Jake went from the garage to the house. The next door she tried opened to a huge laundry room. She thought she'd lived in a large house, but this one took size and luxury to a new level. Although she didn't actually know what the laundry room in her old house looked like. She must have seen it on the original house tour, but she wasn't even sure about that.

Countertops in the same gray and white granite as the kitchen lay above a side-by-side washer and dryer with enough buttons to launch a ship into orbit. She was glad she didn't have to figure out how to run the things. She froze. Laundry was probably on her list of duties as housekeeper. Rats! She'd figure that out later.

Right now, she was a woman on a mission, and that mission was to clean a room for a grandmother who was due to arrive the next day. A grandmother who would spend each day in the house. A woman she hoped wasn't overly observant and didn't follow country music.

She gathered what she needed, then went out the side door to the living space and up the stairs. She loved Jake's design choices. The living room had the same wood beams as the kitchen, this time spanning the width of a vaulted ceiling.

She followed the hall to the right until she found the elevator door, which had a keypad lock on it. It must be for safety, but she was going to have to know the code if his grandmother needed help using it.

She went into the room next door and stopped in the doorway. Sunshine streamed through windows with white gauzy curtains, and a floral bedspread covered a sturdy antique-looking four-poster bed. Rugs scattered about on the wood floor were in soft, muted pastels of pink, green, and blue. This room was unlike any other she'd seen so far in his house, so she knew Jake had it decorated for his grandmother. Her heart caught. The man must have some flaws, but she hadn't found any yet.

She quickly pulled back the covers and stripped the bed. She had no idea if these were fresh sheets or from the last visit, so she would replace them with new. There must be a linen closet somewhere in this house.

She threw the pile of sheets outside the bedroom door. The next door to the right opened onto a small sitting area with two cozy wingback chairs in a pink and green floral pattern, a small, soft green couch and a TV.

On the opposite side of the hall, she tried a door which led to another guest room with a private bath, one decorated more like her room. The door at the end of the hall netted her a walk-in linen closet. She stepped in and found a section of the shelves that seemed to apply to his grandmother's room. She seriously doubted that Jake would be sleeping with pink sheets or using floral towels anytime soon.

She grabbed a full set of clean linens, returned to the room, and made the bed. Curious about the view from the window, she looked out on the backyard and noticed dust on the windowsill. She had more work to do.

She had never minded work, though. It gave her time to think about other things, and the thing that often came to mind at those moments was music. The sun streaming in the window made her think of "Sunshine Cowboy." Marta would probably be here by now, but in the kitchen on the other side of the house and downstairs. There was no way she would hear anything.

Charlotte did a little bit of a warm-up then launched into "Sunshine Cowboy" at the top of her lungs, just as she would on stage. With the dusting done and the carpet vacuumed, she went into the attached bathroom, also decorated beautifully in the same colors. Jake's designer, presumably the one he'd dated, had done a great job.

Small glass jars with pretty ceramic tops in the same pastels sat at the back of the bathroom counter. Charlotte hung the towels she'd brought from the closet over the empty towel bar.

Sun streamed through a window set high in the wall over the bathtub. Charlotte grinned and started in for another verse of "Sunshine Cowboy." She came to the end of the song as she finished wiping down the floor. Then she stood and rubbed the small of her back.

"Wow!"

She whirled around. "Oh my gosh, Jake." She put her hand on her chest and leaned against the bathroom counter. "You scared me. What are you doing here?"

"I turned around about halfway to my office and came back for my briefcase. As I walked by the stairs on my way to the home office, I heard music. I came up to see how you were getting along in Grandma's room, thinking you were playing music to keep you entertained while you worked. I discovered *you* were the source of the music."

"The sun streaming in the window made me think of that country song," she said, hoping Jake had never heard it before. She was the only one who had successfully done a cover of it.

"I don't know anything about country music, but you should be able to make a career with a voice like that. Shouldn't you?"

She chuckled. "Oh, ye who know so little about the music industry. Talent isn't always all that's involved. You need three things: a great voice, a special charisma that helps you stand out—star appeal—and a willingness to work hard. And I don't like to call anything luck, but meeting the right people helps." To herself, she added, *you'd better not know the wrong people who might rob you blind.*

Jake watched her with a curious expression on his face. "You intrigue me, Charlotte McDaniel. But I'd better get to work. I have a meeting in a couple of hours, and I need these papers there." He patted the side of his briefcase.

She watched him leave, wondering if she'd gotten herself in deeper than she'd realized. What would he say when he learned the truth?

Jake went through the upcoming week in his mind as he entered his office building. Stepping inside the elevator, he pushed the button for his floor, and the luxurious surroundings had him smiling. Not for the first time, this reminded him how quickly he'd gone from a single office in a so-so location to two floors in the best building in the city.

The doors opened to his executive assistant with a notebook and pen ready. Harriet's first words were, "Your meeting at ten moved up a half hour."

"Good morning to you too, Harriet."

"Good morning, sir."

"Any updates on the Music Inn project?"

His always in control assistant winced. "The plumbing has to be redone."

Jake stopped. "Wiring, roof, *and* plumbing? And we just got started."

"Yes, sir."

"I need to get over there." He turned back toward the elevator.

She placed her hands on his shoulders and gently pushed him toward his office. "You need to sign some papers, take the meeting, *then* you can go out."

He did as she'd directed. "You're right, of course. What about the small house in East Nashville?" When he'd been over there helping to hang drywall, it had seemed to be on track.

"Going well." She smiled. "You do know that you could turn a tidy profit on it?"

As he entered his office, he said, "Yes, but affordable housing is hard to find in Nashville. I'll make sure it sells to a good family for a reasonable price."

"I'm sure they'll appreciate it."

Harriet had become his office mom, and he'd told her that often. "Thanks, Mom."

She grinned. "In other news, human resources has two engineering candidates they believe will work. After we almost hired someone with a sketchy past last month, you told me to ask you this: background checks before or after interviews?"

He blew out a breath. "Let's do it after this time. It still feels like an unnecessary intrusion if we aren't going to hire either of them."

Harriet gave him a look that said he was being a softy again. "As you wish."

And that brought him to his personal situation. He took out his phone. "I need you to contact Mitch and Charlotte, my new employees at home, and run background checks." He forwarded their contact information to her.

The more he got to know Charlotte, the more it felt like a betrayal to ask for a background check, but he had to because of Grandma. Charlotte was probably so used to that being part of a job application that she wouldn't give it a second thought, anyway. But it had seemed to bother her.

CHAPTER SEVEN

*C*harlotte stepped out of the laundry room and heard a doorbell. When she went out to the main living area, the sound lessened, so she turned toward the kitchen.

A parcel delivery company, who must have the gate code, had a package for Jake which she signed for. A moment later, Marta came in with herbs in her hands.

"I planted a small herb garden this spring. Basil and sage today." She rinsed the herbs at the sink.

"They smell heavenly. I know you're busy, but I wondered if there was anything I could eat for lunch."

Marta turned to her. "Always. Chicken from last night. Maybe a salad?"

"Perfect, thank you."

Charlotte fixed her lunch. When it was ready, she started to sit at the island, then decided to eat by the pool. She'd only seen it in the dark.

The rectangular pool with a waterfall at the end and a hot tub beside that made a beautiful lunch view. A covered porch at this end of the house met a screened porch at the other end. She sat in a chair at what would be an outdoor dining table.

Her life right now felt too good to be true. Yes, she was cleaning someone's house for a paycheck. But he was nice to her, and it was a gorgeous place to live.

Mitch stepped outside of his pool house unit wearing old jeans, a T-shirt, and sneakers. He must be ready to go to work.

"Did you get something to eat yet?" Charlotte called out to him.

"I had some food I kept in an ice chest at my other place. I'm moving up because there's a small fridge in here." He looked up to the sky. "It's a scorcher today."

"That's why I'm in the shade."

"I won't have any shade where I'll be working today."

"What did Jake say he wanted you to do when you talked last night?"

"His grandmother is coming tomorrow, and it seems she likes pretty, girly colors. He wants a couple of pots of bright flowers next to the front door, one on either side. I'm going to get those first. Then I'll check the rest of his front garden beds to make sure everything looks okay."

"Let me take you upstairs to show you his grandmother's bedroom. I think that will tell you a lot more about the colors she likes. I assume it was decorated to her tastes."

As they entered the side door, she introduced Mitch to Marta over the sound of a running mixer, then they went out the kitchen door.

"It's strange even to me, but I'll miss that dump of a motel. I knew the long-term residents. We used to play poker in one guy's room some afternoons. Other than practicing, musicians don't have a whole lot to do in the middle of an afternoon."

Charlotte laughed. "No. We don't."

"Aw, so now you do admit you're a musician." He looked at her, expecting an answer to his unspoken question.

"I told you I'd done a lot in music. I have."

"Ever sung on stage?"

She felt trapped by this line of questioning. She'd managed so far by not actually lying, and she'd continue that way. "Yes, I've sung on stage. I'd like to do more of it. But I also liked helping you with your music the other day."

He grinned. "I sang that song last night. And I got way more applause at the end than I ever have before. If you want to help me with a couple more songs, I would love that."

Jake hadn't seemed too happy to find her in Mitch's unit last night. She wasn't sure why, unless he didn't like a relationship between employees. Not that she felt even the tiniest bit of attraction to Mitch. He was a nice guy and easy on the eyes, but he wasn't her guy.

"Maybe when you've worked outside for a couple of hours, and you need a cool air break, it will be time for me to take a break too. Actually, I started really early, so it will probably be the end of my day then. I assume Jake won't be home until five thirty or six."

After a quick trip to Jake's grandmother's room, they both went back to work.

Time passed pretty quickly for the next hour. She vacuumed the downstairs and dusted. Then she cleaned the downstairs powder room. The public spaces in the house, to her untrained eye, seemed ready for company.

Upstairs, she tried two new doors, finally finding Jake's room at the opposite end of the hall from his grandmother's.

Twice as big as any other room, it had a very masculine feel with stainless steel furniture and clean lines. She went into the master bath and found that once again it topped the house she'd owned. Done in a color scheme of black and white, it had a steam shower, a gorgeous freestanding tub, two separate vanities, and two large walk-in closets. The man knew how to do luxury.

She got it all into shape. Then, considering her day to be reasonably complete, she sat down in the living room to wait for Mitch. She wouldn't use this room when Jake was home, but she really didn't want to invite Mitch into her bedroom and give him the wrong idea.

Closing her eyes, she leaned back on the couch. She'd always thought that performing was strenuous, and it was, but every muscle in her body hurt right now. She didn't think any exercise could have prepared her for the last few days. When the job ended, she'd probably be ready to sign up for a triathlon.

Her phone rang and an unfamiliar number showed. "Hello?"

"Charlotte McDaniel?"

"Yes?"

"This is Jake Anderson's assistant."

Charlotte gulped. The background check had been done.

She continued. "I'm calling to let you know it came back clean. As I'm sure you expected."

Even with the dreams she'd had, Charlotte didn't realize until that moment how much she'd worried about this. "Thank you. Yes, I knew I hadn't broken any laws."

They ended the call and Charlotte leaned forward, taking in steady breaths. Should she just tell Jake? How mad could he be? Yes, he'd hired a famous person to clean his house. But she'd needed the money and had done the work. The problem was that she still needed the money and doubted he'd keep her as his housekeeper if he knew who she was.

Marta brought Mitch in with his guitar. With the background check behind her, she hoped she'd sleep better tonight.

After an hour of music, Charlotte felt invigorated, and Mitch had a grin on his face.

"Tonight's gig will be awesome!" He tilted his head to the side and looked at her. "My band is pretty good. Would you like to be there?"

Charlotte had a feeling he was asking her a bigger question than the one about the concert. Just in case he wanted more than friendship, she gave a mature answer, one that made her seem too old for a younger man. "Thank you, but this has been a busy day. I want to be quiet and relax."

"Let me know if you change your mind."

"Jake's grandmother arrives tomorrow. I may need to rest up."

He laughed. "I'm picturing a sweet old lady with a cane. She's wearing a flowered dress and bakes cookies as soon as she gets here."

The doorbell rang, and Charlotte jumped to her feet. She followed Mitch toward the kitchen. But when the bell rang again, she realized that the sound was different from earlier.

"See you later, Charlotte?"

"Absolutely," she said as she swiveled on her heels and headed for the front door, smoothing down her hair as she went and checking her clothing to see if she was neat enough to greet a guest. When she looked through the peephole in the door and didn't see anyone, she pulled aside the curtain on the side window. A petite woman, she guessed probably in her 80s, was standing on the porch.

Opening the door, Charlotte said, "May I help you?"

"You are?"

"The housekeeper, ma'am."

Charlotte eyed the woman in front of her. She was wearing the velour tracksuit that was not uncommon with her generation, this one in a deep jade color. A few sequins were scattered on the front of the jacket that was over a matching T-shirt. Her sneakers were silver. Her hair was short, gray, and nicely cut. All in all, she looked like a put-together mid-eighties-plus woman.

"May I help you?" That sounded like proper housekeeper-ese.

"I'm Shirley." The woman leaned back on her heels like that should mean something to Charlotte.

"I'm sorry, Shirley. Mr. Anderson isn't home right now. If you'd like to leave a message for him, I'll tell him you stopped by when he gets home from work."

Shirley pushed on the door and barreled past Charlotte. "You're pretty, but maybe not overly bright. I'm his grandmother."

Well, shoot. Charlotte had messed that one up for sure. Tick off the old lady, and you'd probably tick off the grandson.

"He said you would be arriving tomorrow. I'm sorry, but I hadn't been expecting you, and I've never heard him call you anything but Grandma."

Shirley put out her hand and Charlotte shook it, feeling the older woman's firm handshake. "As I said, I'm Shirley Miller. And you are?"

"Charlotte McDaniel, ma'am. If you have bags, I can help

you carry them upstairs, or you could sit and relax and wait for Jake to arrive." As soon as Charlotte said the word "Jake," his grandmother's eyes lit up. She never should have called him by his first name. The woman didn't say anything, but she eyed Charlotte differently than she had moments earlier.

The older woman went into the living room. Charlotte noticed two suitcases on the front step, so she brought them inside. "I think I would like to sit here and relax a bit. Why don't you sit and join me?" Grandma sat down on the couch and patted the cushion next to her, smiling at Charlotte in a cunning way.

She would have to be wary of this woman. Society said that people in their eighties weren't as sharp. She'd long suspected that wasn't true, and this woman was certainly proving the point.

As Charlotte sat down, she said a short prayer. She might be out on her ear in the next ten seconds if this woman did not approve of her, and she hadn't gotten off to a good start.

Charlotte pulled out her phone. "I'll ask *my boss* what he'd like us to do."

"Nice save, honey." Grandma leaned back against the cushions.

She fired off a text to Jake, her fingers flying on the keypad as she explained that his grandmother was early and here in his living room. When no reply came, she knew he must be driving or in a meeting. Or the poor man could just be in the bathroom.

She set her phone beside her, hoping for a ding, something that would get her out of this situation.

"Your room is ready for you, ma'am." She hoped the older woman would take the hint and go upstairs. She'd probably come down later for dinner with her grandson.

Disappointment washed over Charlotte when she realized that if Grandma were eating with her grandson, the help probably wouldn't be. The housekeeper would be back in the kitchen at the island. Maybe outside, but if he wanted to sit by the pool with his grandmother, she'd be banned from there too. She'd always been able to go anywhere she wanted, but now she was the help, and people in those positions stayed behind the scenes.

Ding. Charlotte picked up her phone. She read his text and groaned inwardly. "Mr. Anderson says he is unavoidably detained." *No!* "And will be home in about an hour. He asked if I could take you upstairs to your room or help you with anything else you wanted to do." She raised her eyes to look at the older woman.

"I think I will go upstairs. Jake told me he'd had a security system installed on the elevator after he read about the danger of home elevators and children. One of his Boston friends brings his kids when he visits. Do you have the elevator code?"

Charlotte shook her head. "No, ma'am."

She pointed at her right side. "Hip replacement surgery a few months ago. It doesn't slow me down much, but stairs are still a challenge."

"Maybe you'd like to watch TV?" Charlotte glanced around and realized she didn't see a TV.

"How long have you worked here?"

Charlotte decided that being straight about where she'd been working before she came to Jake's house was definitely the best policy with this woman. Trying to put a more professional shine on it wouldn't work. "I started working as his housekeeper yesterday. Before that, I was cleaning in a motel his sister recently bought."

"Lizzie? What's she done now?" The woman shook her head. "She has a way of having everything come out smelling like roses, both of them do, but she gets herself into some fixes every once in a while. Is Jake helping her with something?"

Stepping into the middle of a family situation fell into the category of never go there. "I think it's best if Mr. Anderson explains the situation to you when he gets home."

Grandma rolled her eyes. "That answers it. Lizzie's in trouble again, isn't she? And don't put me off with that 'my boss will tell you' thing. If you have the answer, spill."

Charlotte chuckled. "Okay, the story *as I know it to be*," and she emphasized those last words, "is that Lizzie bought a motel sight unseen, right as she was heading out of the country to go to Bali to do interior decorating for someone for a month."

The woman laughed and slapped her knee. "That's my Lizzie. She's the one who takes the most after me. Life somehow turns out well for her, though. Jake's helping fix it, isn't he?"

When Charlotte hesitated, Grandma added, "There's no need for you to tell me. It's obvious that he's helping her. That's where he met you, and that's how he got a housekeeper for his home. Am I getting warm?"

"Hot as a cup of coffee."

His grandmother lowered her voice and looked around, almost as though she expected someone to overhear her. "That other cleaning woman he hired, he seemed to think a lot of her, but the house wasn't overly clean."

"Okaay." Charlotte dragged the word out slowly. "Did you tell him that?"

"Honey, I don't step in the middle of my children's or grandchildren's lives. It isn't my business."

Charlotte had to bite her lip not to laugh. This woman seemed like she jumped in the middle of everything that came in her path.

"He's been a good employer. The job's new, but he seems fair. In regard to using his first name, which I believe you caught on to . . ."

Grandma nodded slowly.

"He told me that we met under unusual circumstances at Lizzie's motel, and he saw me more as a friend first."

"Is that so," his grandmother said with a knowing expression on her face.

Rats! Well, instead of making it better, she may have made her situation worse. Now Jake was clearly fraternizing with his employee. Maybe if she could change the subject to something that was on safer ground. "Do you live very far from here?"

"Florida. The Miami area."

Grandma explained about her house, her two dogs that she'd boarded while she was gone, but in a place they loved, and the restaurants she enjoyed there. Instead of being boring, though, she was entertaining. Charlotte occasionally commented because she had been in the Miami area, but she'd seen it as she usually saw travel destinations, from a tour bus and then a stage. She heard Jake coming in from the garage.

As soon as he entered the room, he shouted, "Grandma!"

Shirley patted Charlotte's hand and said in a low voice, "That was a good distraction, dear. I knew you were trying. But I did enjoy talking to you."

Charlotte grinned. "Can I adopt you?"

Patting her arm again, Grandma said, "I'll consider it. And please call me, Shirley." Then she stood.

Jake hurried over and gently put his arms around his grandmother, pulling her close. "It's so good to see you, Grandma." He held her at arm's length. "But I'm sure you said you were coming tomorrow morning. I've even cleared the day of work, so we could spend your first day here together."

"You've met Charlotte?" He smiled widely at Charlotte, his grandmother following the move. "You should hear her sing, Grandma. I walked in on her this morning."

"You clean and sing? That I want to hear. What kind of music?"

"It was country music, Grandma. I'd never heard the song before, but it was upbeat."

"You'll have to sing for us, Charlotte."

That was the last thing she wanted to do. She wouldn't be surprised if this woman were a huge country music fan. She looked like she could get out there and do some boot scooting on the dance floor too. "I think that right now I'm more of a sing in the shower kind of girl. Mr. Anderson happened to catch me singing while I cleaned. Hardly a performance." She laughed, but it sounded more like a panic attack with laughter underneath.

Jake seemed to be missing the undercurrents between her and his grandmother. She liked the woman. She really did. But Shirley saw something more than was really going on between her and Jake. Charlotte felt like the older woman knew she wasn't what she was pretending to be. The irony of it all was that as every hour passed, she became more and more of a skilled housekeeper. What would the tabloids do with that?

CHAPTER EIGHT

*J*ake took his grandmother and her luggage up in the elevator. He said the code out loud for Charlotte as he punched in each number, and she entered it into a note on her phone. At least there would never be that excuse again for having to be alone with Shirley.

Charlotte went to her room and checked her hair, running a comb through it, then freshened up her makeup. The soft pink lip gloss and blush wouldn't have been much makeup a couple of weeks ago, but this was her new look.

When she stepped into the kitchen at dinnertime, she found Marta preparing dinner plates.

"You have enough for Jake *and* his grandmother?"

She laughed. "I want him to be able to invite someone to dinner at the last minute. I always make enough for four or more." She picked up two plates and walked toward the kitchen's swinging door. "Mr. Anderson told me he'd like to eat by the pool."

"It should be nice out there." And Charlotte wished she could enjoy the evening by the pool too. She set a place for herself at the island.

Before Marta returned, Jake stepped into the kitchen. "Marta brought two plates. You're eating with us, right? I thought we solved that this morning."

"But your grandmother is here. I'm the housekeeper."

Jake smiled at her in a way that melted her knees. She gripped the side of the island to hold on. Wow, that man could smile. "I'd like to have you join us. I think you'll enjoy getting to know my grandmother. Oh, and if you're thinking about staying away from dinner, my grandmother said she enjoyed her chat with you and would like to have the opportunity to talk to you more." And then he was out the door.

And Charlotte was stuck having dinner with a highly inquisitive, razor-sharp older woman.

Jake watched his grandmother and Charlotte chatting. They seemed to be getting along well. He loved his grandmother, but he didn't think he made her laugh as much as Charlotte was right now.

She looked at him, then over at Charlotte and back at him. Jake wasn't sure he liked the speculative glance.

Then again, he could deflect any grandmotherly matchmaking. He needed to stay far away from any employee, or he could end up in a court case that could ruin more than his wallet. It could take his reputation too.

A close friend had gone down in flames when his

secretary had reported a getaway with her boss to the media. She'd been fired for unrelated reasons, and was angry, but the weekend had been anything but forced on either's part. The dirt had stuck, anyway.

"Grandma, what do you want to do while you're here?"

"I've visited several times since you moved to Nashville. We've always done a lot of family things. This time, though, your sister's out of the country, and your parents won't be back for a few days, right?"

Jake nodded slowly. He wasn't sure where this was going, but he'd told her he had tomorrow off. And he could probably sneak away for some time with her in the following days. He waited for her to continue the conversation because he knew his grandmother would say exactly what she wanted.

"I'd like a tour of Nashville."

Charlotte scooted forward in her chair. "Is there something special you'd like to do, Shirley?"

At what point had his grandmother and his housekeeper switched to a first-name basis?

"Well, Charlotte, I'd like to see something to do with music. This is Music City, USA, right? Jake moved here three years ago, but I haven't experienced the music. Unless you count the canned music that plays in a restaurant."

Charlotte laughed. "No. I wouldn't count that."

Jake stepped into the conversation before his grandmother sent his week completely out of control, and he found himself taking days off at a time when he already had a full schedule.

"How about visiting the Ryman, Grandma? It's a historic building and periodically hosts Grand Ole Opry events.

Sometimes with a drummer named Steve." He gave Charlotte a smile that said he remembered her story. "I took some business associates on a backstage tour last year, and they loved it. A tour guide shows you into the dressing rooms and talks about the famous people who sang there."

Charlotte put her hand on her chest, and her eyes grew big. She gulped. Did his new housekeeper hate country music? No, that wasn't right, because she had been singing country music. At least it had sounded like country to him.

His grandmother clapped with glee. "That sounds perfect, Jake! Can we go tomorrow?"

"I'll go online and see if we need to have reservations."

Charlotte looked down at her plate of food then up toward the pool and off to one side, before releasing a raspy sigh. She did *not* want to go on that tour. If she told him why she felt that way, he wouldn't ask her to go. She had a mysterious air to her like there was a story. He wanted to know that story.

He wasn't ready, though, to figure out why he cared. He pushed his chair back and stood. "Anyone like a swim?"

His grandmother yawned and patted her mouth with her hand. "Oh my, no, that's for you young people. I think I'll just go up to bed. I've got a great book, and you know how much I love to read."

The last part was true. The first part was an outright lie. His grandmother swam laps several times a week at her community pool.

He knew he'd lost control of his grandmother's visit when she turned to Charlotte and said, "We would, of course, want you to come along to the Ryman, Charlotte. I've enjoyed our visit tonight. I do love my grandson, but it's nice to have another woman along." She looked up at Jake, almost daring him to dispute her decision. She knew full well he never would.

Charlotte said, "Fine," in a tone that suggested she'd rather do almost anything else. "I'm not interested in a swim tonight either."

His grandmother jumped in again. "Of course you are, Charlotte. You had a long day cleaning, right?"

Charlotte nodded slowly. Then she rubbed her right upper arm. That must be one of the places where she was feeling the strain from days of scrubbing.

"Then a swim is exactly what you need. I'm going to wait here until the two of you young people get your suits on and get in that pool." With a determined expression, his grandmother leaned back and crossed her arms. "There are suits of all sizes in the pool house."

Jake looked at Charlotte and shrugged. They stood and he went toward the house. Charlotte surprised him by heading toward the pool house. He had to give her credit for being fast on her feet. Grandma didn't realize Charlotte lived here. It might be best if she didn't know for now.

Trunks on, he returned to the pool and found Charlotte already in the water, standing there really, not splashing around. She was talking to his grandmother and seemed to have relaxed some from their earlier discussion about the Ryman.

As soon as he arrived, his grandmother got to her feet. "You two have a nice swim." She smiled a little too sweetly and yawned. "I'll go read my book before I go to sleep." She hurried inside.

His grandmother leaving him alone with a woman was out of character. He sat on a lounger. What did he do now? Alone with his beautiful employee? He soon heard the click of a lock and looked up as light spilled onto one of the porches above him—his grandmother's porch to be exact. That sneak was spying on the two of them. They weren't alone.

He wouldn't give his grandmother a show. He'd treat Charlotte as he would Lizzie, like a sister. Maybe that would be the end of her matchmaking. What was she thinking? His housekeeper appeared to be a down-on-her-luck musician, and Grandma was trying to match them up? What was it about grandmothers and making sure their grandchildren were happily married?

He cannon-balled into the deep end of the pool, splashing water high and in every direction. Charlotte screamed as the water hit her.

She whirled toward him. "I'm going to get you!" She dove under the water and came up beside him, then shoved him to the side. "I grew up playing in pools, Mr. Anderson. If you act like a kid, I'll treat you like one." She dove under, grabbed his two legs, and pulled them out from under him.

He rolled over and came up spitting water. "You're in trouble now!"

She swam fast to the other end of the pool, but she wasn't fast enough. He shoved a wave of water over her head and she came up sputtering.

"Truce?" She coughed.

He raised his hands. "Okay. Truce."

She glanced around as though she should get out of there, anyway.

"Don't worry. I'm always true to my word. Did you want to swim laps or just lounge in the pool?"

"Lounging sounds good to me. You didn't clean a bedroom, a bathroom, another bedroom, another bathroom, a living room—" She slapped her hand over her mouth. "I'm so sorry. You're paying me to do that. You don't want to hear me whining about the work."

He laughed. "I may be paying you, but that doesn't mean it wasn't work. You're a hard worker, Charlotte, and I appreciate that. I'm going to get a couple of rafts, and we can just float around on the water. How does that sound?"

"Heavenly." She sighed.

Floating on the raft a few minutes later, he heard the snick of the door lock and looked up. His grandmother must've gone in for the evening. If she continued matchmaking, he would have to have a chat with her. As long as Charlotte was his employee, any hint of a relationship was one hundred percent impossible.

Charlotte stared up at the starry sky as she floated in Jake's pool. How had her life changed so abruptly? Not that long ago, she'd been everybody's darling. She'd made the cover of dozens of magazines over the years. The tabloids had loved her, often when she dated a man they assumed would be her forever love. None of them had been, but that didn't stop them from reporting it.

And now she was floating on the water in a gorgeous pool, staring at the stars with a handsome man not far away. Of course, she was his housekeeper. Only and always. He'd made that distinction quite clear.

Her life had changed so much. Tears stung her eyes. She blinked rapidly so that they wouldn't fall, but one escaped and rolled down the side of her cheek. She would find a way to be a star again.

She turned her head to look over at Jake. The tour at the Ryman could be a deal-breaker. Maybe they only told stories about iconic singers from long ago. But she kind of had a feeling that the story of her singing when the power went out was worth telling.

78

CHAPTER NINE

*C*harlotte rose bright and early with a surprising amount of energy, and decided to get a head start on their breakfast. She found a container in the freezer labeled "blueberry muffins." She licked her lips. "Yum!"

"What's yum?" a female voice she knew well by now asked.

"You're up early," Charlotte said to Shirley.

"I could say the same about you, Charlotte."

"I'm the help, ma'am. I'm supposed to be at work before anyone else is up."

"And you know that to be true because . . ."

Charlotte thought about the best answer to Shirley's unusual question as she put three muffins on a plate. "Shouldn't the housekeeper get up before anyone else?"

Shirley sat on one of the stools at the island and plunked a laptop down in front of her. "I can't help you with that, my dear. Even now, I only have someone who comes to clean a few hours a couple of times each week." She leaned closer to

Charlotte and lowered her voice. "And she *really cleans* twice a week." She shook her head and rolled her eyes.

Since the older woman was taking her into her confidence, Charlotte had to assume she meant her own cleaning had been of a good standard. That made her feel happy inside. She always liked doing things well. If someone said she needed to practice her guitar for an hour, she'd do an hour and a half or two.

As she was about to ask how the older woman had slept, Jake pushed open the door to the kitchen. This time he'd dressed in shorts and a T-shirt with the logo for Nashville's football team, the Titans.

"You're looking rather touristy today, Jake," she said.

He laughed. "That's the look I was going for. I thought if we were doing something touristy, I'd put on my one T-shirt that says 'Nashville.'" He turned to his grandmother. "If it's okay with you, Grandma, we can go to the Ryman and do the tour this morning. I got tickets online for the three of us. After lunch, I'll bring you back here. I have a last-minute meeting this afternoon, and I'd really like to be able to handle it. Then I can spend most of tomorrow with you. Will I be shirking my duties as your grandson if we work it that way?"

"That's fine, Jake. Business is what pays for this beautiful house." She flipped open the laptop. "Let's see what we can do during the rest of the week." Shirley's confident tapping of the keys surprised Charlotte.

Jake watched Charlotte and smiled. "She was a computer coder for decades."

"Wow." This was a sharp lady. And Charlotte was going to the Ryman, the heart of Nashville's musical roots, with her. Uh-oh!

Charlotte was on edge when they arrived at the Ryman. But by the time the tour started to wrap up, she was having fun. She'd always enjoyed stories about the old-time greats like Johnny Cash.

The final stop brought them to the wings of the stage. How many times had she stood in this very place waiting to take the stage and sing her heart out?

Jake said, "Charlotte, you ought to step out on that stage and sing that song of yours."

Charlotte froze. If he mentioned the words, this was over. There was only one "Sunshine Cowboy," and that was her song. Their tour guide would put the pieces together.

The guide laughed. "If I had a dollar for every time someone said they needed to get out on that stage and sing to prove themselves . . ." He shook his head. "I'm sorry, ma'am, you may have a fabulous voice, but there's no one here to hear you right now and make you famous."

Charlotte giggled. She couldn't help herself. It would never occur to her to get on that stage right now and sing for a contract. This was Music City, and that meant that thousands of people came here hoping for that dream. She'd been one of them.

"I *would* like to walk out on the stage, though. Would that be okay?" The tour guide waved his hand in that direction, so Charlotte did, more memories flooding her mind with every step. She stopped in the center. At the risk of sounding a little bit crazy, even in her head, instead of seeing the empty seats in front of her, she saw them filled with people, even the seats to the far left and right where concert-goers could barely see the stage.

They were chanting "Carly" over and over again. And then she began as she always did with "Sunshine Cowboy." Would that memory hold her for a lifetime? Was that enough? Did she get to hold on to her title of country music star forever?

She breathed in a raspy breath, pasted on a smile, and turned back to the group. "I'm ready to go now. I've had my moment in the limelight."

"You looked good out on that stage," the tour guide said. "Something about you reminded me of an incident that happened here, oh, about five or ten years ago, I think it was. One of the big stars, a country music queen I haven't heard much from for a couple years, was out on that stage belting out a song, and the crowd was lapping it up. Right in the middle of it, a thunderclap sounded, and the lights went out."

Would this not only be the end of their tour but also her time with Jake?

"You could hear the rustling through the audience as they were trying to figure out what to do. Then the security lights popped on. She didn't miss a beat. She deserved the title of country music star. That Carly Daniels was something. A real lady."

Her heart racing, Charlotte looked at Jake and his grandmother, who showed no signs of recognition. Their guide led them back through the building and out to the foyer, where they could wander around and look at the photos and memorabilia on display. As they started to walk away, he added, "There's a photo of her that night on the upper mezzanine's wall. You may want to check it out."

Charlotte gasped.

"Are you okay, Charlotte?" Jake asked her, resting his hand on her arm.

She nodded vigorously. "Yes, I am. I think I may be hungry, though. Yes, very hungry." She trilled a laugh, hoping for a beautiful sound, but it came out like she was coughing.

"Well, that's up to Grandma. Do you want to walk around the building more, Grandma?"

His grandmother stared at Charlotte. "No, I think I'm getting a little hungry myself. Is there somewhere good to eat around here?"

"I thought maybe we'd have some barbecue today. But I don't remember, Grandma, do you like barbecue?"

"Is Florida humid? Of course I like barbecue."

He glanced toward Charlotte. Her heartbeat was slowing down to a more normal pace, now that she knew they wouldn't be staring at her photo in the next few minutes. "I love to eat. There isn't much I won't eat. And if it has something to do with the South, I probably love it."

As they walked away, Shirley asked, "Even banana pudding?"

"Even that."

Shirley shuddered. "Cookies and pieces of banana in vanilla pudding somehow cross a line for me. I'll let you eat that alone. But I'll take a slice of pecan pie any day of the week."

Both Charlotte and Jake laughed.

Shirley stopped at a display loaded with tourist activity brochures and scanned them before reaching for some. "I'm grabbing everything musical."

Great, Charlotte thought. *Just great.*

When they'd almost finished lunch at a nearby restaurant, Jake checked his watch. Charlotte noticed that it appeared to be very expensive—gold with what were probably diamonds surrounding the face. "I have a meeting at two, so I have plenty of time to take both of you home, or I can drop you off somewhere else if you'd like to continue sightseeing."

"I need to get back to work, Jake."

He brushed her comment aside with his hand. "I'll leave that up to my grandmother."

Shirley looked up from the piece of pecan pie she'd been enjoying. "I think I'd like to rest this afternoon. But I want to look through that material on Nashville to choose something for us to do tomorrow."

Jake picked up his phone and flipped through his schedule. "I have a meeting at three." He scrunched his face as he studied it. "I don't think this is one I can easily move. I think I'll have to let you and Charlotte plan something to do in the afternoon."

Charlotte sat back in her chair. Was she a housekeeper? Or was she his friend who was hanging out with his grandmother?

"That will leave you a couple of hours this afternoon to get some cleaning in, Charlotte," he added.

Or maybe she was both.

"Could the three of us eat outside again tonight, Jake?" Shirley asked. "It should be a nice evening."

Jake's concerned glance in Charlotte's direction made her wonder what was going on.

"I bought tickets for a concert for the two of us over a month ago, Grandma. I checked this morning, and they're sold out. Sorry, Charlotte. And I've already given Marta the day off."

"I don't mind a quiet night at home." And she meant that. She wouldn't have to pretend to be someone else.

He gave her a heart-melting smile of thanks. When he dropped them off at his house, he walked his grandmother inside, then left. Charlotte continued with her in the elevator up to the second floor and then to her room.

With Shirley settled, Charlotte got her tools of the trade out of the laundry room and did a quick clean of the downstairs living area and the dining room. Then she made Jake's bed and replaced his towels.

How often should a housekeeper bring fresh towels? All of these unknowns. She might have to go online. There was probably a YouTube video: Housekeeper 101. She took her bagged trash to the trash can next to the garage.

CHAPTER TEN

*M*itch was outside, pulling some weeds from one of the planting beds.

"Working over at the inn later?"

He stood and stretched. "The roofers are up there right now, and they keep throwing things off the roof, including old nails. It seemed like it was best for my long life if I stayed away for a few days. Maybe when they finish one end of the building, I'll be able to go back. Mr. Anderson has quite a bit of work to do here, though. It wouldn't be a reach for me to spend days weeding and getting things straightened up."

Mitch glanced at the ground, frowned, then leaned over and pulled out a weed he must have missed. He cocked his head and looked at Charlotte. "I have a buddy coming over to visit this afternoon, another musician in my band. Would you be willing to work with the two of us on something?"

She'd had quite a bit of fun doing that. It felt good to be useful in music. She didn't get paid for it, but fun was worth something, wasn't it? A little voice in the back of her head told her, "It doesn't put food on the table." She ignored that little voice, though, because right now, she had all the food she could eat. She'd have to figure out her future sometime, but in the meantime, she'd learned that she could be a decent housekeeper. She was a natural.

"When could you come over? Mr. Anderson's grandmother will be resting upstairs. I don't think she would hear us if we were in the main living area. And he'll be home in a couple of hours."

"Andy and I have about an hour. We're playing a gig tonight."

An older sedan drove up the driveway and stopped at the end.

"Mr. Anderson said I could give Andy the gate code since he'd be over here practicing."

A blond man about the same age as Mitch got out of the car. Then he reached in and brought out an acoustic guitar. These were her kind of people.

Mitch waved him over. "Andy! Come on over here and meet Charlotte."

Holding his guitar, Andy glanced around the backyard. "You've done well, Mitch."

Mitch laughed. "It's a great gig."

"Hey, you said Charlotte? You're the one who helped Mitch with his song. Can you—"

She held up a hand. "I've already agreed to help. If Mitch wants to finish what he's doing and wash up, then bring your guitars in the side door, and find me in the living room."

When they sat down on the two chairs that Charlotte had set in front of hers so she could watch them easily, she said, "Play just the instrument first, then I want to hear the lyrics too." That had always helped her with a new song.

"Yes, ma'am," Mitch said.

She listened to the guitar music all the way through. Then she circled her finger in the air, and they started again, both playing and singing. When they finished the second round, she sat back and said, "Very nice. I've never heard that before. Is it yours?"

Andy nodded. "What do you think?" He scooted to the edge of his seat as he waited for her reply. "I haven't played it in public yet."

"It's good." She knew how to make it better and decided to take a risk for these guys. "I think adding a female voice in the mix could turn it into a hit. I'll sing with you to see how it would work."

"You're a singer?" Mitch asked.

"I can carry a tune."

Mitch watched her closely, but Andy spoke first. "That would be awesome!" He started the song again, and Charlotte joined in, singing quietly at probably a third or half of what she was capable of for volume and intensity. When they got to the end, she said, "Nice. What do you guys think?"

Andy looked stunned. He shook his head as though to clear it.

"It never occurred to me to add a girl to our group," Mitch said. "It seems ridiculous, but we've just been guys playing music. Your voice made all the difference. Charlotte, would you join our band?" He looked over at Andy, realizing that he might have spoken too soon.

Andy nodded his head. "Yes, please, Charlotte, join our band."

"I appreciate the offer. But I have a dream of singing on stage alone with a backup group behind me. I don't think I want to be part of a band, even if it's an awesome one. But," she added to the two men now wearing disappointed expressions, "I could change my mind. I doubt it, but let's have some fun."

"Yes!" Andy pumped his fist. He started the song again, this time with the confidence he lacked earlier.

Charlotte jumped in with gusto, staying close to her normal volume. A startled Mitch watched her, and she realized she may have made a critical mistake. If his parents had been country music fans, he might have grown up with the voice he'd just heard.

"You sound familiar."

"Maybe I just have one of those voices." Charlotte laughed. It seemed like she'd been living on fake laughter the last few days. If it sounded as bad to everyone else's ears as it did to hers, she must seem like the biggest phony on earth.

She usually had confidence. Maybe a little too much sometimes, because she'd been called demanding. Sure, she wanted to get things right. It had taken her a while to learn the difference between perfection and excellence. You can be excellent and not be all crazed and wrapped up in being perfect.

Andy looked hopeful when he asked, "Can we sing it one more time? You haven't offered any new direction for the song. I was hoping for that after talking to Mitch."

"I like it the way it is. I think that the song can grow and evolve as you practice it. I've seen that happen many times. But let's give it another shot."

"Let's get it right this time," Andy said. "Everybody just sing as though you're in front of a crowd." He put his guitar strap over his shoulder and connected it on the bottom, then stood. "Let's pretend we *are* a group."

"What's your group's name now?" Charlotte asked.

"It wouldn't work with a girl. There are two more men, along with the two of us. We're the Four Cowboys."

"I actually like that. If you find a girl to join the group, you could be the Four Cowboys and a Cowgirl or A Cowgirl and her Four Cowboys."

Andy laughed. "That would be great. Our country music often has a retro vibe to it, and that name fits. I grew up with country on the radio. The kind of songs that are often sad because a girl left, and they have a lot of alcohol in them."

Charlotte laughed, relieved to hear it sounding natural this time. Then she stood up along with Mitch. Tapping her foot, she found the rhythm. "Ready, guys? One, two, three."

Andy started to play the song, and all three of them sang at a performance level. About halfway through, they started to get some dance moves. When they finished, Mitch and Andy did a fist bump, and each took turns hugging Charlotte.

Clapping came from the other side of the room. They all turned to look at the source, Charlotte praying that it was Marta who had stopped by on her day off.

Shirley Miller stood there grinning from ear to ear. "You're an amazing group. Can we go hear you tonight?"

Charlotte felt the room start to spin. She held on to the side of the sofa to stay upright. She'd had a good run of it.

"You could come to hear Andy and me tonight," Mitch replied. "It sounds so much better with Charlotte, though. I wish she'd join us. We have a great gig playing over at a club on Lower Broad."

That was about the last place on earth that Charlotte would show her face. She'd been discovered at one of those clubs.

"You guys have fun," she said. "I wouldn't be surprised if you found somebody to join your group right there tonight."

"They won't be you, though, Charlotte." Mitch frowned.

The guys each hugged her again before going in the direction of the kitchen and the side door.

Shirley walked toward her. "Jake was right. You *can* sing. Did you come to Nashville for music?" She sat down on the sofa.

No lies. Charlotte would not lie to this woman. She liked her too much. And she also liked herself too much to lie. Skirt the edge, yes. Bald-faced lie, no. "Yes, ma'am. I came to Nashville with stars in my eyes." She restored the chairs to their original places. Then she sat on one that faced Jake's grandmother.

"So you worked in music here in Nashville." There wasn't a question mark at the end. It was a statement.

"Yes, I did. I thought I was going to have a great career in it. Things haven't gone too well lately."

"And that's how you ended up in that dump of a motel that Lizzie bought?"

Charlotte laughed. "That's how. I guess Jake took you by to see it?" She tried to think of a time they hadn't all been together.

"He showed me pictures. He said it might be too dangerous to visit until more of the work is done."

"Yes, Mitch, the dark-haired man, is going to be doing the landscaping there. He has a degree in landscape architecture. But he said that while the crew is working on the roof, there's too much flying debris for him to want to be anywhere near it."

The older woman nodded her head once. She seemed to

be glad that her grandson had been honest with her. "Will you stay home alone tonight, Charlotte?"

"Yes, ma'am. I sometimes enjoy a quiet evening."

"It must be terrible living in that motel of Lizzie's while all of this is going on."

Charlotte flipped through the Nashville travel brochure and answered without giving it much thought. "That wouldn't be very pleasant. I'm grateful that I have a room here in the house."

"Excuse me?" There was a chill in Shirley's voice that hadn't been present thirty seconds earlier. Charlotte glanced up. What had she just said that seemed to upset her? She went back over her words. Nothing stood out. "Did I say something that bothered you, ma'am?"

"You, an unmarried woman, have been sharing the house with my grandson, an unmarried man? Both of the same age, both seeming to share an attraction for each other?"

Charlotte felt her face grow hot, and she knew she was blushing from the roots of her hair to her toes. She sat up straighter. "He's my boss, Shirley." She used the familiar name, hoping to calm her down. "It's a room off the kitchen that was designed for a housekeeper." She pointed to the left. "His room is upstairs and down the hall." She gestured toward the stairs. "If you're thinking we're shacking up, I hadn't even seen his room until I cleaned it. And I doubt he could tell you the color of mine."

His grandmother shook her head. "I don't like it. I don't like it at all. No fooling around?"

There was something about having any sort of sexual conversation with someone of this age that totally freaked Charlotte out. "No, Shirley. He's my boss."

"He's handsome, though, isn't he?" She watched Charlotte carefully.

"He is that. I can't argue with the truth. He's handsome, kind, and seems to like to laugh."

"Only around you, my dear. He's been a mess since Evangeline took off."

She had to bite her tongue to not ask about Evangeline. That truly was none of the housekeeper's business. Besides, with the Internet, she could probably look up his name and Evangeline and get all the information she wanted. Of course, she wouldn't do that, would she?

Now that Shirley knew she lived there, maybe the matchmaking would stop.

Charlotte excused herself, got her purse, some money from the envelope, and headed to the grocery store up the street for some tools of her cleaning trade. On the way, she changed direction and went to Radnor Lake to walk and relax first. Wow, did she need that.

Jake sat in his car, facing the gate.

"I don't think we're going anywhere with that truck in the way, Jake," his grandmother said. "I don't want to miss the concert."

A huge utility truck with the electric utility's name emblazoned across the side was blocking his driveway. They probably shouldn't do that. Then again, when they needed to repair something, they might not have a choice.

"Can you call one of those new taxi-like companies?" she asked. "Or a limo. That would be nice."

His car's clock told him they didn't have time to call for a ride. An idea came to mind, so he dialed his housekeeper.

When she answered, he heard loud noise in the background. "Charlotte, can you hear me?"

"Just a second, Jake." She paused. "Now I can. I stepped outside the grocery store. Do you need something?"

"Could you pick Grandma and me up and take us downtown to the concert?"

Silence greeted him. "Charlotte?"

"Why? You have many cars."

"A utility truck is parked in front of the gate. I think they're fixing a power line. We have," he paused to check his watch, "just enough time to get to the concert if you're at the store up the street."

She jumped in before he could say any more. "I'm a couple of blocks away. I finished shopping and have a cart of groceries inside that's ready to go through the checkout line. I'll be there in a few minutes."

He sighed. "Thank you!"

He let his grandmother out so she wouldn't have to walk far, then backed up the car and returned it to the garage. He hurried back down the driveway and opened the gate in the metal fencing with a key. As they walked through it, Charlotte pulled up behind the large truck that had a bucket raised to the power line across the street.

He swung her truck door open, and it let out a horror-movie-worthy screech.

"Great truck, Charlotte," were his grandmother's first words, but she said it in a positive way.

Jake put his hand on his grandmother's arm. "I'll help you inside, first."

"I'm not old. I can get in there myself. You go first." Her

stubborn expression communicated her feelings well. He hesitated, but Shirley stood her ground. "Didn't you say we were in a hurry?"

He hopped inside, then extended his hand for his grandmother.

She did get in the truck with little effort. Settling in, she sighed. "They don't make them like this anymore."

Jake snorted.

"Hey, it's a classic." Charlotte patted the steering wheel.

Jake's arm brushed hers as he buckled his seat belt. Every nerve in his body tingled. He ignored the warmth of the female body next to him. Or tried to.

"Where's the concert?" She put the truck in gear. "I'm assuming downtown, so it's this direction."

"It's at the Schermerhorn. The symphony center is beautiful, but there aren't as many seats as some other venues. I am sorry that they didn't have a ticket available for you today."

"It's no problem. Even if I have to park on the street, I'll be able to watch a movie or read a book."

His grandmother leaned forward. "Or sing?"

"I'll leave most of my singing as cleaning entertainment."

His grandmother patted his arm. "Isn't a man in a tuxedo handsome, Charlotte?"

"Almost always." Charlotte glanced his way.

So that's why his wily grandmother had pressed him to wear a tux to a venue without a dress code. She'd wanted to impress Charlotte.

"Isn't it nice sitting next to Charlotte, Jake?"

His muscles tensed. Matchmaking again. She'd wanted them side by side. No wonder his grandmother had turned down his offer of boosting her into the truck.

Charlotte kept her focus on the road and the evening traffic. He felt her warmth every time she turned the steering wheel. Every single time she moved, her warm body pressed against his.

"Grandma, please roll down your window for some fresh air."

"Feeling warm in here?" she asked.

He wouldn't touch that comment.

"We're almost there," Charlotte said. She pulled into the drop-off area, put the truck in park, and hopped out.

After opening the passenger door, she held out her hand. "I'll help you down, Shirley." His grandmother started to speak, but Charlotte stood there without wavering. Instead of mentioning what would probably be a sensitive comment about her agility, she said, "You're petite, and it's a long drop."

Charlotte impressed him. She hadn't mentioned age. After helping Shirley down, she stood back for him.

Shirley hugged her. "Thank you, Charlotte."

Jake jumped down from the truck and closed the door. "I'm sorry again about the tickets."

"No problem. That is a nice tux. Have a great time."

CHAPTER ELEVEN

*A*s she drove away from the Schermerhorn, Charlotte smiled. Shirley had gotten one thing right; there was something about a man in a tux. Especially that man.

With the driveway now clear, Charlotte drove in and spent a luxurious evening at home. After a long bubble bath —the liquid from a container on the counter along with shampoo and conditioner she hadn't used—she dressed in her oversized sleep shirt. Her fashionista best friend Maggie would be appalled. But Charlotte was more about comfort when it came to sleep. And there wasn't anyone else to see it.

After drying her hair, she sat on the side of her bed. Shirley had made her think that Jake and Evangeline had a story.

She scrolled through her phone. A search of Jake Anderson and Evangeline brought up a stream of photos of the two of them. They seemed to have been society favorites in Boston a few years ago. One article alluded to her coming from old money, that may have fallen on hard times.

No one knew why the romance had ended. But there was

a dramatic video of Evangeline tugging the engagement ring off her finger and throwing it six feet toward Jake. When the ring looked about to hit him on his cheek, he blocked it, and it flew out of camera view. Jake moved to Nashville soon after.

As Charlotte did a little more digging, she found a photo of Evangeline's wedding in Boston a year later to a wealthy man about twenty years older and nowhere near as handsome as Jake. But she did look happy in the photo.

Then there was Jake. The man lived alone in a different city. She had to guess that Evangeline had broken his heart.

Charlotte threw back the covers then stopped and put her hand on her stomach. She'd had a lot of meals lately where she'd only picked at the food. Today's lunch was one of them. She'd had a light salad for dinner. Being constantly on edge, wondering if you were going to be exposed as a fraud, could weigh on you.

Sometimes she wished everything would be revealed, and she could just go back to being herself. But who was she now? A country music star? As the days passed, she felt a little less like one. But when she worked with Mitch and Andy, she felt like her old self. Only better.

Tomorrow, she'd tell the truth. Jake might just laugh. They didn't have any connection beyond employer and employee, and she'd clean just as well as she had before.

She pulled on her robe and tied the belt. Then she headed for her door to see what she could forage for a snack. This was a very well-stocked kitchen. She knew she'd seen some corn chips and bean dip in a cupboard earlier today. She'd grab that and take it back to her room. She stepped out into the kitchen and headed for the cupboard without turning on the overhead lights.

Faint light, enough to see by, shone through the window from outside. She loaded her arms with her booty, including a soda from the fridge. This was not her most nutritious snack, so she ripped a banana off a bunch.

Turning with her arms full, she walked straight into someone.

Charlotte screamed and jumped backward. Everything in her arms hit the ground with a thud.

"Charlotte, what are you doing here in the middle of the night?"

As she looked around for something to use as a weapon, it sank into her mind that this person had called her by name.

"Jake?" she said with a not-too-weaponlike roll of paper towels in her hand.

"Who did you think it was? I came down for a snack."

"Me too. I hope that loud crash and my scream didn't wake your grandmother."

"You haven't eaten much since she arrived. Is she causing you that much stress?"

"No, absolutely not. She's great. It's just some personal stuff I've been going through." As she bent down to pick up her treasure trove of snacks, Jake leaned over to help her. Their heads hit, and she fell to the floor.

"Ouch!" She held her head.

"Charlotte? Are you okay?"

She groaned. "Uh-huh."

"Are you sure?"

"Yes. I was really looking forward to having the corn chips and dip, but I think I just sat on them."

He chuckled. "Let me help you up. You're in a minefield of kitchen supplies."

She knelt on the floor, waiting for his help.

"I held out my hand to you, but you can't see it, can you?"

"Not down here. Let me try it on my own." When she started to stand, she stepped on the can of bean dip, which rolled, attempting to take her down again. Struggling to find the solid floor, she stepped on the banana and her foot slid. Jake must have had enough light to see her plight because he grabbed her with both arms and held on.

So that's where she found herself when she caught her breath, with Jake holding on to her. As warmth flowed into her, she looked up into his eyes.

"Thank you for catching me." Her voice had a breathy sound.

He touched the side of her face. A gentle touch.

A sigh escaped her and he softly kissed her lips. Her heart danced, and she felt like bursting into a sweet love song. As her eyes fluttered closed on their own, she slid her arms around him, pulling him closer, and he deepened the kiss.

Suddenly, there was a blinding light. This must be the fireworks people talked about.

"Nothing between you?" an outraged voice said.

Jake raised his head and looked directly into his grandmother's angry eyes. Not just angry, but disappointed in him. The anger he could take. The disappointment . . .

"It's not what you think, Grandma! This didn't mean anything."

He felt Charlotte gasp against him, and he knew he'd said the wrong thing. He'd disappointed his grandmother, and now he'd hurt Charlotte.

"She told me she was just the housekeeper. I got pretty much the same story from you. You know how I feel about single people and things going too far before marriage." She waved her hand around, generally pointing at the two of them still standing much too close together for housekeeper and boss.

And that's when his grandmother's words sank into his head. He was Charlotte's boss. He had just kissed his employee. The kiss had been spectacular, but this could be the biggest mistake of his life on so many levels.

"Jake, it's okay. I know this didn't mean anything." Charlotte looked at his grandmother. "I know you won't believe me now, Shirley, but this truly hadn't happened before." Stepping over the flattened bag of chips, she started walking toward her bedroom door. "I'll get my things and be out of here in the next ten minutes."

As she reached her doorknob, she glanced back at him, and the overhead light caught the glint of tears running down her cheeks.

His grandmother walked over to Charlotte and put an arm around her.

Okay, so now he had Charlotte crying, his grandmother angry and disappointed in him, and a potential lawsuit on the horizon. At least this night couldn't get any worse.

Staring at him defiantly, his grandmother said, "Jake, you've disappointed me."

This was *much* worse.

She'd been on his side all his life. The reality of his housekeeper's situation crashed in. Charlotte might not have anywhere to go.

"Grandma, could you leave Charlotte and me alone for just a few minutes? I think we have quite a bit to talk about."

She planted her feet firmly and looked stubborn.

He added, "Please?"

She turned and marched out of the kitchen, but he had a feeling she'd either be back very quickly or be listening at the door. Maybe both.

He walked over to Charlotte and spoke in low tones, words soft enough that he didn't think his grandmother would be able to overhear them. "Charlotte, I'm sorry about what happened."

She looked up at him and knuckled away the tears on her cheeks. "Sorry about what, Jake? That you kissed me or that you were caught kissing me?"

He shook his head. "No, you don't understand. That was wrong of me as your employer."

"I thought you were my friend," she said, more tears filling her eyes.

He was outnumbered. A grandmother and a housekeeper, two females, were angry and glaring at him.

He put his hand on Charlotte's cheek and brushed away tears with his thumb. He felt her suck in a breath. The seed of a wild idea came to him and quickly grew. How far was he willing to go?

～

Charlotte's heart leaped in her chest. She wanted to memorize every angle of Jake's face, his smile—except he wasn't smiling now. He looked more upset than anything. She wouldn't get to explore her feelings for him anymore, though. She would be spending the night in her truck.

"Charlotte, I think I have a plan." He lowered his voice even more. "Something that can get us out of this mess."

Did he have a plan for having her stay in his life? Her heart raced as she thought about more kisses from this man.

"If you're willing to pretend to be my fiancée . . ."

She froze. *Pretend?* She realized that Jake's lips were still moving. "Please repeat what you just said."

"I said, if we pretend to be engaged, you keep your job, Grandma is happy, and"—he hesitated, so there must be another reason—"everything will be fine."

The man seemed to be missing a few critical pieces here. She would've thought he was missing a few essential gray cells if it wasn't for the fact that he was an intelligent, self-made billionaire.

"Jake, engagement isn't a short-term solution. It's two people saying rather publicly that they plan to be married, generally at some point in the not-too-distant future. How can that work?"

"You'll be my fake fiancée. We'll act like we're engaged around family."

So this would be a very private fake engagement.

"My grandmother will eventually go home. I don't know when that will be, so don't ask. She stays as long as she wants to, and she doesn't tell anyone in the family how long that will be. When she leaves, we'll simply tell everyone it didn't work out between us. As long as you're here and in the house, you're my fiancée."

She felt like asking what was in it for her. But she was standing in the doorway of a clean, safe, and attractive room with a man who, in general, treated her quite nicely. She had food and time to get her life back on track. Her options narrowed to what might fit on the head of a pin.

"Yes. I will be your fake fiancée."

He grinned, and she wished down deep in her soul that

his grin had to do with the fact that he was thrilled to be engaged to her. But she knew it was because of his grandmother, and something else he wasn't sharing. That was okay. She had a roof over her head for a few more nights.

He hesitated. "I know that you seem to be struggling financially. How about if I give you a thank-you check for fifty thousand dollars when my grandmother leaves? Then you can start over and not have to worry for a while."

She felt anger simmering under the surface. Who did he think she was? Someone so needy they would take fifty thousand dollars from him. But maybe she was exactly the person he thought she was. She could tear it up if she changed her mind. "Thank you, Jake. Now, I think I'm ready to go to sleep."

"No. Now you have to give the greatest performance of your life."

She stared at him, puzzled.

Then he called out, "Grandma?"

The door opened immediately, so Charlotte knew the older woman had been trying to overhear. Jake put his arm around her and held her close to his side as they walked over to his grandmother. He whispered to Charlotte, "Make it good."

Fifty thousand dollars and a home. She looked up at him, intending to have a fake and adoring expression, but her heart melted again because he was looking at her the same way.

"Yes, Jake? Are you going to tell me the truth now?" Shirley stood with her feet apart, her hands on her hips, looking every bit like a drill sergeant from the Army. One you wouldn't want to cross.

"Grandma, I think you would agree that if Charlotte was living here and was my fiancée, then what you saw would be inappropriate while under my roof, but not as disturbing to you. Am I right?"

Shirley glanced from him to Charlotte and back before answering. "Are you telling me that the two of you have been engaged? That you didn't tell me? And that you were going to let this sweet girl, your fiancée and a woman I could immediately tell would be a good match, walk out of here tonight into the darkness?"

Jake smiled and said, "Charlotte has agreed to be my wife."

Charlotte turned toward him, startled. They'd never used the word "wife." That made it seem more real. Somehow, the shift between fake fiancée and wife felt abrupt. Of course, what else was a fiancée in the real world, but a future wife?

He rubbed her upper arm gently, and she felt her insides melt. The unspoken words in his gaze told her to act the part.

She slipped her hand into his and squeezed it. "It all happened so quickly, Shirley." That much was true. She'd gone from someone who struggled to always tell the truth even in this bizarre situation she'd found herself in, to someone who now lived a big fat lie.

Jake kissed her cheek. The man was good. She would've thought every second of this was real if she hadn't known better.

"Of course, Grandma, we want to keep this private, just for the family, right now."

His grandmother glared at him. "Aren't you proud of your fiancée? Are you trying to hide her? And why would that be?" The suspicion returned.

Charlotte felt Jake stiffen next to her. The lie twisted around them.

"I'd like to share our news with my family in person before the public knows. That seems right. Mom and Dad are out of town, and Lizzie's on the other side of the planet. You know we're close, and I'm not sure Lizzie would forgive me anytime soon if I announced that I was engaged, and she couldn't be here to meet my fiancée."

His grandmother gasped. "You haven't known Charlotte long enough for your sister to have met her?"

"This happened very quickly, Grandma. Lizzie was very busy as she was getting ready to head out of town. I didn't even see her for a while. I got a call from Bali about the motel."

Nice save, Jake. Not once did you tell a lie. His grandmother knew he'd gotten a call from Bali about the motel. He just didn't tell her the number of days that had passed since they'd met. There was such a thing as love at first sight, though, wasn't there? Jake rubbed his finger on the top of her hand. Every time he did something like that, she felt gooey inside.

Charlotte could hear the clock chiming in the living room. When it hit twelve, she wondered if her prince would vanish.

They all agreed it was time to go to bed. Again. Charlotte would've liked to start this day over again, forget everything —except for the kiss. Too bad there wasn't a rewind button.

Shirley stood in the doorway. "I'm going back to bed. You're leaving now, too, Jake." She made it a statement, not a question.

Charlotte suspected that his grandmother would barely let the two of them out of her sight for the rest of her stay.

The other night, she'd pushed them to swim together. But then she was just trying to get two people together, and she didn't know Charlotte was living in the house.

"See you in the morning, Charlotte." His steamy gaze roved over her. Then he ushered his grandmother out of the kitchen.

Wow. She would give a year of her musical career to have that man look at her that way every day for the rest of her life.

The mess on the floor reminded her that she needed to clean it up. Sighing, she crouched and gathered everything in her arms. She was still the housekeeper. Nothing had changed, and yet everything had changed.

CHAPTER TWELVE

*C*harlotte caught her reflection in her bathroom mirror as she reached for the spray bottle of cleaner. "Your life is such a mess, Charlotte McDaniel!"

Yes, she had been talking to herself. But life had been challenging lately.

Her life had felt out of control a week ago. "I guess if it's between out of control, broke, and living in a filthy, buggy place, or living in a rich man's house and being his pretend fiancée, I'll take the second option."

Jake didn't want to hurt his grandmother's feelings, so he had proposed. Who did that? Jake Anderson, that's who. Her *fiancé.* Charlotte giggled. She finished cleaning the shower and the rest of the bathroom. Then she got back in the shower to start fresh for this first day as an engaged woman.

Then, wearing her robe, she sat in the chair and sent Maggie a text. *I'm engaged.*

Excuse me? As in busy doing something or planning to be married?

Married.

Her phone rang.

"What?"

"Before you get too concerned, it's a fake engagement."

Charlotte heard tapping in the background. "Maggie?"

"I'm checking flights to Nashville."

Charlotte laughed. "I'm fine. It's temporary. We're making his grandmother happy."

The tapping stopped. "Are you sure you're okay?"

Charlotte gave it a few seconds of thought. "Yes. I'll text updates."

"You do that." She could see her friend's mock stern look.

After they ended the call, Charlotte dressed in her jeans and T-shirt uniform, vowing to never leave her room again without being fully clothed. She found a fully clothed Jake in his kitchen. Actually, the back of him as he stared into the refrigerator. His grandmother was nowhere in sight, and that surprised her.

"Good morning!" She wasn't sure if she should act as she had yesterday morning, as a housekeeper, or if she should somehow act more like a fiancée because his grandmother might be outside the door.

Jake answered her question. "When I walked Grandma to her room last night, she told me she would be sleeping in this morning. It's just you and me. Let's get our story straight."

Charlotte walked up to him and whispered, "Jake, I don't think we should talk about this in the house. We don't know where she is, and we don't know when she's going to appear."

He gave a reluctant nod. "You're right."

"We act engaged anywhere your grandmother may be." She pulled the blender closer. "What's going in our smoothies today?" Charlotte asked in what she hoped sounded like her normal voice, not the sound of a panicked housekeeper and fake fiancée. Oh, and grandma-pleaser.

"Peach. Marta's note says we have strawberry muffins in the freezer." He opened it to check. "Yep. Are you hungry?"

Before she could answer, she heard rustling sounds beyond the door told her Shirley was making her way through the house. The older woman's idea of sleeping in must have been seven o'clock.

Charlotte whispered, "I'd always pictured the morning after I got engaged as having a bit more, I don't know, gusto."

She noticed the footsteps had stopped. Jake seemed oblivious, so she pointed toward the door.

He glanced that way with a questioning expression on his face. For a bright man, he could be dense. She mouthed the word "Grandma."

In a few short strides, he was in front of her. "Good morning, my love." He kept his eyes on the door. When it started to move, he added, "It's always a wonderful morning when you're part of it."

Charlotte felt like giggling. But when she was just about to laugh, he wrapped his arms around her and dipped her back. She reached up and grabbed his shoulders to keep from falling, but he actually had a solid grip on her.

Her nerves kicked in. Even though she'd spent a lot of time performing on stage, she didn't feel comfortable with public displays of affection.

As his grandmother stepped through the door, he kissed Charlotte, his lips gently brushing hers. When she pulled him closer, he brought her upright, wrapping his arms around her and putting her in a lip-lock for the ages.

An unknown number of seconds—or minutes—passed. Then he let go, and Charlotte reached for the island to steady herself. She focused her attention away from him and willed her emotions back in place. This wasn't real. Pasting on a smile, she reached up and touched his cheek gently with her palm. "You can greet me that way any morning, honey."

He turned toward his grandmother and said, "Oh, Grandma, good morning!" The man should have gone for a career on the stage.

Wanting some space, Charlotte said, "Why don't you two sit down in the dining room, and I'll prepare breakfast." When neither of them moved, Charlotte went to the fridge to get the smoothie ingredients. Sure, she'd like another kiss, but he'd given his one show of the day. She didn't dare hope for a second matinee performance.

Another of Charlotte's kisses was all Jake wanted. He took a deep breath, and then another. Charlotte was right. Other than performances like that one—no matter how much he'd like to repeat that kiss—they needed to keep their distance. They *weren't* really engaged.

He liked having Charlotte here, though. She seemed to brighten everything in her path.

He herded his grandmother out to the dining room and pulled out her chair for her. Once she'd sat down, he realized they didn't have any coffee. "Grandma, let me get both of us a cup of coffee."

She smiled oddly and said, "Sure, Jake."

As he walked away, he pondered that expression. When he pushed through the door to the kitchen and saw Charlotte, he realized that his grandmother thought he was trying to find an excuse to see his intended alone. That fit their plan perfectly. Maybe he should call it *his* plan. But the thing that surprised him as he stood in the doorway and watched his *fiancée* work was that he had wanted to see her again. That couldn't be a good thing. *Stick to the plan, Anderson.*

"I don't want to startle you."

Charlotte jumped and put her hand on her chest. "That's the wrong thing to say when you walk into a room, and someone thought they were alone."

He headed over to the coffeepot and grabbed three mugs off of the shelf above it. "What would be the right words to say to someone if they were expecting to be alone?"

She laughed. "Maybe there are no right words."

He filled the mugs, took them to the dining room and returned.

Charlotte poured smoothie mixture from the blender into three glasses. "I guess eating a fairly light breakfast is one reason you have such an awesome body." She turned to look at him and grimaced. "Pretend I didn't say that. *Please.*"

"You think I have an awesome body?" He stepped up behind her, wanting to wrap his arms around her and pull her close, but he resisted. It was just proximity, the two of them spending a lot of time together. In the end, they were housekeeper and employer, and he needed to remember that. Maybe he should talk to a lawyer to find out what the legal ramifications of this engagement could be. Could an employee sue him for kissing her?

He carried a glass and the plate of muffins while Charlotte brought the other two glasses and a stack of plates with silverware on top.

"Do you have anything planned for us to do this afternoon, Grandma?"

She pulled a tourist brochure out of her pants pocket and put it on the table. "I'd like to take a bus ride to the homes of the stars."

Jake struggled to keep a smile on his face. Sitting on a packed bus and looking at houses wasn't his first choice for fun. Then he remembered that he had a meeting. "I'm sorry. I can't go with you, Grandma."

He looked pointedly from his grandmother to Charlotte, who appeared less than happy, almost panicked at the thought of taking this bus ride. He assumed she shared his sentiments about it. She'd been in music for a while. Maybe she'd actually seen one of the stars who owned a house on the tour.

He wondered again about her music background. As his housekeeper, he felt like he didn't need to know details. As a fiancé, it might be a good plan to learn more about her. His grandmother watched him. He realized she needed to keep an eye on them to make sure everything seemed right between them, that her grandson was happy with his "engagement." If he left the house, maybe she could relax.

He picked up his phone and sat next to his grandmother as he searched for and found a highly rated tour company, then made reservations. "You're set. If you come downtown at about noon, I can take you to lunch and drop you off for your tour. Either have Charlotte drive one of my cars or have a car pick you up."

His grandmother patted his hand. "Thank you, Jake."

He stood and headed for the garage. "The tour is booked for two o'clock. Have a good morning."

"Are you going to ask your fiancée what she'll be doing this morning?"

Yeah, he should do that. "You're right, Grandma. I'm still new at this fiancé thing."

"It's not like this is your first time as a fiancé, though, is it?" she said.

Charlotte didn't look too surprised at the revelation when he glanced at her. Maybe she'd done an Internet search of him and read the rumors and stories. Everyone assumed the woman was the wronged party in a public split. *He* must have been the bad guy. But Evangeline had only been in it for the cash she thought he had and would have. He'd still been new to business, but she'd apparently seen potential in him. Evangeline had lied to him when she said she loved him, and about much more. She'd married her sugar daddy, though, and Jake couldn't have been happier when he received news of that wedding.

"I'll be sprucing up the bathrooms, putting out fresh towels for all, changing sheets, and doing a load or two of laundry." She gave him a tense smile.

His grandmother glared at him, and he knew he was in trouble. Before he could say anything about his fiancée not cleaning his house, though, Charlotte spoke up again. "I don't mind doing the work. It gives me something to do. Makes me feel useful. And if I were the wife of anyone but a billionaire, I would probably be doing all of this myself, anyway. And cooking."

He couldn't argue with her logic. After a peck first on his grandmother's cheek, then on Charlotte's, he escaped to the garage, choosing a sedan that would comfortably seat them all later.

He'd always prided himself on having a fairly orderly life. He enjoyed the thrill of the hunt in real estate, finding a diamond in the rough and turning it into something that could sparkle and earn him a lot of money. That took order and not a small amount of creativity at times. But his life seemed to be spinning out of control. On the good news side of the equation, at least no one outside the family would know.

As he pulled into the parking garage under his office building, his phone pinged with a text. He checked it and found one from his grandmother. *Buy the poor girl a ring.*

He leaned his head back against his seat. Evangeline's engagement ring had disappeared. Even if it hadn't, though, his grandmother knew that ring well. She'd been living near him at the time and had been around the two of them frequently. Thinking back to those days, she'd always been polite to Evangeline, but never seemed to seek out her attention.

His grandmother both liked and wanted to spend time with Charlotte. Interesting. He checked the time again. He would have about forty-five minutes after morning duties in his office, before their lunch and his next meeting. He'd recently gotten his watch battery replaced at a very nice jewelry store not too far away, so he'd go there on his break.

Jake neared the jewelry store with a plan in mind. He'd buy a simple ring, put it on Charlotte's finger, and his grandmother would be happy. It had to suit Charlotte, though, be one she might choose, or it would raise a red flag to his grandmother. His steps slowed as the store came into view.

If the media caught wind of this relationship, it would be everywhere in a heartbeat. It would go viral on social media. When he'd been called one of the most eligible men in America in a major publication, it made his love life worthy of note. After attending social events three times with one woman, speculation had run wild. To stay under the media's radar, he'd made sure to never date the same woman more than two times. Unfortunately, to those who followed such things, he now seemed more intriguing, not less.

His plan would change when he met the right woman.

In front of the store next door to Josephine's Jewels, he stopped and glanced around, not seeing anyone he knew or who seemed to be observing him. Another step and he glanced around again.

Then he realized he looked so ridiculously obvious that he'd been right to not pursue his childhood fascination with private investigation. With one last glance over his shoulder, he stepped inside the store.

Apparently, when you came to a jewelry store at eleven in the morning, you had the place to yourself. He'd need to remember that in the future.

Glass cases filled with jewelry formed a large square, and an older man in a suit stood in the middle of the square.

"May I help you, sir?"

Jake swallowed. The last engagement ring he'd paid for had been what Evangeline and her mother had chosen and pointed out to him. It had screamed money, but he was only starting to find his way in business then, and paying for it had been a stretch. Now he could buy anything in the store.

"I need an engagement ring."

The man looked Jake over from top to bottom and got a big grin on his face. A custom-tailored suit and diamond-studded watch seemed to bring out the best in salespeople.

"This way, sir." The man led him to a case at the far end of the store with two plush chairs in front of it.

"I'd like something very simple."

The man's expression became a little less happy. He unlocked the case and brought out some rings that had a few small stones set in them. "Maybe if you tell me a bit more about the lady, then I'll be able to find the perfect ring."

Good idea. Jake breathed out a sigh of relief. An expert was on the job. "She likes bright colors, but she's not flashy. Brown wavy hair, green eyes." He tacked on the only career information he knew. "Oh, and she's worked in music."

The man looked from Jake to the tray of rings in front of him and back at Jake. "Let me get something a little more unique for the lady. Musicians often prefer the unusual and creative."

Charlotte couldn't be described as a musician, could she?

This time the man brought out rings that were still simple but had a few more twists and turns in them. They seemed a little too feminine to him. Not that Charlotte wasn't feminine in every way and in everything she did, but these weren't her style.

"Too fussy."

The man set those rings back in the case and stepped away to a different case. While he was gone, Jake studied the case in front of him. A ring covered with a cluster of random shapes and sizes of stones in different hues of pink, blue, and yellow said Charlotte to him.

The man returned with another tray of simple rings, exactly as requested. But Jake pointed out the ring in the case.

As the man took it out, he said, "I don't think this is what you're looking for, sir. Perhaps the lady would prefer one of these rings." He put his hand on the edge of the tray of rings he'd brought.

Jake picked up the multi-colored ring and slipped it onto the end of his pinky, the only finger it fit on.

"The stones are all naturally colored diamonds, set in 18 karat yellow gold."

"It's perfect. It suits Charlotte to a T."

The man told Jake the price with hesitance in his voice.

"Do you have a ring box to put it in?" Jake asked.

"Yes, sir!" He stepped away and returned with a teal velvet box he slipped the ring into. Jake had always wanted to present an engagement ring to a fiancée in a jewelry box. Evangeline had put the ring on her finger in the store.

This was exactly what he wanted. For Charlotte.

He paid for the ring, and the man handed it to him in a small bag with the company's name on the side. As Jake walked toward the door, he realized that coming out of a jewelry store with a bag in his hand might not be the best plan, but the box would be too bulky for his pocket. He turned around and also bought something for his grandmother—a pendant that had a musical note dangling from a chain, to commemorate her musical tour of Nashville. He asked the sales assistant to put everything in a larger bag.

Few people were out and about when he left the store. He'd made the trip without anyone noticing his jewelry store shopping.

Then one of the city's free buses that shuttled visitors from one tourist destination to another pulled around the corner. The bus stopped at the light, and a woman about his age shouted out the window, "Buying jewelry for a lucky lady?"

Half the bus raised their phones to the window and snapped his photo.

Jake cringed. One more reason to avoid becoming a PI in the future. He and stealth did not go together.

If he could avoid having his life exposed and going viral again, that would make him very happy.

CHAPTER THIRTEEN

*T*he morning went by quickly. Charlotte was just finishing up cleaning Jake's shower when the lunacy of her situation tickled her funny bone. A giggle escaped, then another and another. She held on to her sides and slid to the floor. Sitting in the almost-clean shower, she was grateful he seemed to favor natural cleaners, so she didn't have bubbles scrubbing her backside.

"What have I done?" She leaned against the glass wall. "At least I don't have a ring, a wedding gown, and a venue chosen for the wedding." She was a *fake* fiancée.

When it was time to meet Jake for lunch, she called for a ride. Driving one of his cars didn't seem right. She wasn't a real fiancée, and housekeepers probably didn't drive their employer's luxury or sports cars.

They arrived at the tall tower where his company apparently leased two floors and went inside. His grandmother knew exactly where she was going, so Charlotte just trailed along slightly behind her.

When they stepped off the elevator, the receptionist

looked up and said, "Shirley Miller! It's so good to see you again." The woman disconnected her headset and hurried around to Shirley, giving her a big hug. "Jake said to send you right in when you got here." She glanced over at Charlotte with a curious expression.

Charlotte deflected it with a simple reply. "Charlotte McDaniel. A friend of Jake's."

The woman maintained her professional air, but her curious expression deepened. When would she learn not to use his first name in public? Shirley hooked her arm through Charlotte's and led her away, whispering, "Almost a nice save. Dear, if you and Jake want to keep this a secret, you might have to do better than that."

When the woman was right, she was right.

Shirley introduced her to Jake's assistant, Harriet, as they walked by her into his office where they found Jake on the phone and seated at his desk, looking out the windows. The office had a magnificent view of the city, and she could see forested green hills off in the distance. That was something she loved about being in Nashville. You lived in a city, but could find nature nearby.

Jake ended his call.

"Hello, Grandson."

He spun around. "Grandma!" He hurried over and hugged her. In an aside to Charlotte, he whispered, "Close the door."

When he released his grandmother, he reached into a bag on his desk and pulled out a small, velvet, teal jewelry box. He hesitated but then walked over to her with it and went down on one knee.

Charlotte gasped and covered her mouth with her hand. He opened the box. The most beautiful ring she'd ever seen sat nestled inside. Her heart raced, but as she was about to reach for the ring, she realized. . . This was all part of the act. Part of the show for his grandmother. And Charlotte was nothing if not a show woman. She took a deep breath and let it out slowly. Then she said, "Jake! It's gorgeous! When did you ever find time to buy it?"

Jake's expression shifted from the tentative one of a man on his knee proposing, which was charming, to one where he also seemed to realize he was putting on a show.

"Try it on, honey. See if you like it."

Just when she thought the man was a good actor. That was a cheesy line from a 1930s black-and-white romance. And not one that had ever done well in the theaters.

She reached out and took the box from his hands, holding it in front of her with an excited expression—at least she hoped it was. She took the ring out of the box and tried it on her finger. It fit well.

This wasn't an ordinary off-the-shelf kind of ring.

"Not a diamond, Jake?" Shirley asked.

"These are all diamonds in different colors, shapes, and sizes. I thought it suited Charlotte."

She liked pretty things, but she wanted them to be a bit different, not the same as her mother had worn. She moved her hand from side to side, watching the diamonds catch the light from above.

His grandmother caught her arm. "Gorgeous, Jake. You've done well, Grandson."

Jake rose to his feet. An expression passed between him and his grandmother that Charlotte didn't understand.

⁓

His grandmother clearly approved of the ring, but the circle of gold added more solidity to their relationship. He understood now that the situation would become harder to undo every day they remained engaged.

As they were leaving his office, Jake turned back and grabbed his briefcase. The good news about his meeting was that he didn't have to ride around on a tour bus. The bad news was he wasn't sure the guy was really going to sell, so it might be a complete waste of time.

He followed his grandmother and fiancée out the door, down the elevator, and to his car. As he pulled onto the road, he said, "It made sense to me to eat very close to where you're going to catch your tour bus. I'll have my meeting and come back to wait for you. I can work in the car if the bus hasn't returned yet."

His grandmother spoke up. "Does the restaurant we're going to have pecan pie, Jake?"

Jake chuckled. "You're in the South, Grandma. If dessert is on the menu, there's a very good chance pecan pie will be there. If it isn't, I'll find a place that has it, and we'll get pie to go."

"I like that idea," Charlotte said. "Let's have some pecan pie for dessert tonight."

"It's a plan." He could see her grin out of the corner of his eye. "I know an amazing meat and three close to where we're going."

"Three what?" Shirley asked.

He chuckled. "It's a kind of restaurant in the South, often cafeteria-style. You choose the main course—the meat—and sides. Here in Nashville, sides are often called vegetables even if they're mac and cheese or fruit salad."

This time Charlotte laughed, a sound he loved to hear. "Skip the salad I'd planned to have. I love meat and threes."

Grandma settled back into her seat. "I enjoy trying the local food."

Jake pulled into the restaurant parking lot. They went inside and ordered. His grandmother loved getting sweet tea when she was in the South, so she had that and he and Charlotte had unsweetened tea. They each chose fried chicken as their meat, and mac and cheese as one of their sides.

His grandmother scooped up a bite of the green bean casserole she'd chosen for another side. "I may need to walk around the block this afternoon, but I am enjoying my sweet and fried Southern lunch."

"Agreed." Charlotte sat back in her chair. "I'll be ready for a salad at dinnertime."

As they were walking over to the tour bus office, Jake carrying a box with a pecan pie inside, his phone rang. Charlotte took the box from him, and he moved back a step so he could talk to the caller.

The call was quick and easy. The man canceled his meeting. "Are you sure?" Jake asked. "We could move the meeting if today isn't good for you. No, I understand. Keep me in mind if you change your mind in the future. Thank you." He tucked his phone back into his pocket.

His grandmother, with her supersonic hearing, asked, "Your meeting is canceled?" Her voice held a little too much glee for him.

"Yes, Grandma. But that's okay." He smiled at her, hoping to distract her. "I'll find plenty to do while you're on your tour." He turned and smiled at Charlotte, who raised one eyebrow at him and had an expression close to a smirk on her face.

His grandmother sped up. "Let's see if we can get you a spot on the bus."

Jake hoped all the way across the street that there would be no extra seats.

Charlotte went over to take care of the arrangements. She returned waving three tickets. "Isn't this fortunate, Jake? They had someone cancel, or there wouldn't have been space for you on the bus with us." She grinned from ear to ear.

He could tell she was about to burst into laughter.

And that was how he ended up sitting on a tour bus to see the music stars' homes. He seemed to be the only man on the bus wearing a business suit. He was definitely the only one clutching a briefcase in his lap.

He sat next to the window with Charlotte at his side, at his grandmother's insistence, and her across the aisle.

Charlotte seemed nervous. She chewed her lip, then gave several deep sighs.

At one of the houses, Charlotte leaned over and whispered something to his grandmother.

His grandmother laughed and said, "Really?"

Charlotte nodded at her.

"Okay, what did I miss?"

"It was kind of a girl thing. About that house." Charlotte pointed in the direction of the last one.

"How do you know anything about that particular star's house?"

"Um, I know people who have been there. If you'd like to know a secret about the master bathroom, I can tell you."

Just when he thought he was going to learn something about her, she seemed to find a way to answer him but not answer him. He had a feeling she wouldn't lie to him, though. She just evaded answering.

"Have *you* been in that house, Charlotte?"

She stared at him. Then she took a deep breath and let it out. "Yes. I went to a party there."

"It seems to me that only A-listers would be at a party at one of these mansions of the stars."

The normally happy Charlotte turned sad. "To appease your curiosity, let me say that I used to hang out with some of the country music A-listers."

He knew she was somehow not quite who he thought she was. Not her personality—she seemed genuine in every way. She was caring. Kind. She'd taken great care of his grandmother. But there was something about Charlotte McDaniel that didn't seem right. She'd passed the background check, but that didn't give her life story.

His grandmother was watching them, so he held Charlotte's hand. She glanced up at him quickly and he nodded toward his grandmother.

When they were nearing the end of the tour, the guide described the dining room in the current house, saying that it had red walls, an imported crystal chandelier, and a fireplace taken stone by stone from a castle in Europe.

Charlotte leaned over to his grandmother and whispered something. Then she leaned over to Jake. "It's royal blue."

"Is that an important detail? Maybe they've just painted it, and now it's red?"

"No. It's her signature color. She's still wearing it on stage, so I seriously doubt she'd change the color in her house."

Why was this woman cleaning his toilet? She'd been in some of these houses. Who was his housekeeper?

She squeezed his hand in excitement as she pointed out something in a neighboring yard. He realized that he may not need to know who she was. He was enjoying the moment too much to care.

~

After a poolside meal that night, Charlotte relaxed as sunset colored the sky.

Shirley broke the silence. "Charlotte?"

"Umm-hmm." A slight breeze moved the leaves on the trees, and she released the tension she'd been holding since that bus tour. She'd had so much fun playing tourist that she'd revealed far too much to Jake and his grandmother.

"Charlotte, do you have a vision for your wedding?" Shirley asked. "What you want your dress to look like?"

Like a needle scratching across a vinyl record, she felt her happy mood breaking. She sat upright and returned to the present moment. "I don't have any ideas about a wedding or a dress."

Glancing first at Jake, then at Charlotte, Shirley said, "Jake, please get my laptop. I searched online this morning and bookmarked a few sites."

Jake sighed.

Charlotte read his mind: when can we stop this charade? She twisted the new ring on her finger, wondering the same thing.

He went to do as asked. When he returned, he said, "Grandma, Charlotte's newly engaged. Can't dress shopping wait?"

The man didn't understand the way women thought.

"My research told me there's a long wait time for custom dresses. Charlotte deserves the best, right?"

His grandmother knew he couldn't argue with that. Charlotte bit her lip to stop the laughter bubbling inside her. Leaning closer to Jake, she whispered, "It doesn't cost to look, right? I'll be noncommittal."

He smiled at that and whispered in her ear, "Thank you. Humor her for now."

"Move over here next to me, dear." Shirley patted the cushion next to her, and Charlotte scooted over beside her.

A half hour later, a deer caught in the headlights sensation came over her. A-line, ball gown, mermaid, off-the-shoulder, sweetheart, length of train . . . the list of options went on and on. "So many dresses. How does a woman choose?"

"It does seem overwhelming." Shirley closed her laptop. "I'll need to do more research."

Charlotte wanted to put an end to the older woman's wedding dress obsession. Looking at photos wasn't a problem, though, and it made Shirley happy. As long as they never went dress shopping, her dress searching would be harmless.

CHAPTER FOURTEEN

*D*uring breakfast the next morning, the whirlwind known as Shirley Miller made an announcement. "Charlotte has an appointment at a bridal salon at ten o'clock."

Charlotte held back a sigh. She was caught between the grandmother and the grandson.

"I hope you enjoy *looking* at dresses."

She'd do her best to honor Jake's repeated request to look and not buy an unneeded wedding dress.

She was startled to find a limousine in the driveway when Shirley directed her to step outside the door, but she dutifully climbed inside. Apparently, this was how Jake liked to live. At least when his grandmother was around.

She sat next to Shirley and shifted in her seat as she tried to come up with a plan. He could afford the dress, but it would be one more problem to solve when they split up.

She had a feeling his grandmother would be interested in the very expensive ones. Oh, not because she was someone who wanted to spend her grandson's money. No, because she wanted to give her new granddaughter-in-law the very best.

Dresses were all custom when you watched those TV shows. Could you return a custom wedding dress? There must be off-the-rack wedding dresses, ones you could just walk in and buy in your size. But she had a feeling that wasn't where the limousine was taking them today.

Watching out the window, she saw landmarks for the Green Hills area of Nashville. She knew there were quite a few bridal shops here because she'd seen them as she'd gone to area restaurants. And it was one of the city's high-end areas.

They neared a shop she had never noticed. But then again, she hadn't wanted a wedding dress. She still didn't.

"Do you know anything about the place we're going to, Shirley?"

"Yes, dear. I searched online, and this is the one reviewers liked the most."

How many men had octogenarian grandmothers searching online and checking reviews? Probably not too many.

The chauffeur drove to the front of the building and stopped, leaving the car idling so they stayed cool. Then he walked around and opened the door for Shirley first. Charlotte scooted over and stepped out the same door. To herself, she said, *Let's get this show on the road and get it over with.* To Shirley, she said, "I hope this turns out to be a day you'd want for Jake's bride-to-be." She forced her mouth into what she hoped looked like a smile.

Think. Think. Think. What can you do, Charlotte, so that he doesn't have to pay for a very expensive, probably nonreturnable wedding dress? Nothing immediately came to mind. They went into the store and were greeted by their salesperson, Camille, who first greeted Shirley, the woman who had booked the appointment.

"And you must be Charlotte McDaniel?"

"Yes, ma'am. I'm Charlotte." Charlotte glanced around the room with wedding dresses lining the walls. So many dresses.

"Let's sit over here and chat for a moment." Camille gestured toward a navy blue sofa. "We can figure out what it is that you're looking for and how to best serve you today."

Charlotte had always loved excellent customer service, and it seemed as though this store would deliver exactly that.

When they'd been seated, Camille asked them what they'd like to drink and brought them the water they requested. Then she began asking Charlotte questions.

"What style do you have in mind?"

"This is the first time I have ever in my life looked at wedding dresses." Something she could add that was true came to mind. "Not a red-carpet dress, please. I want it to look like a wedding dress."

Camille gave Charlotte the eye. "Okay. We can get an idea by simply looking around the shop to see which ones catch your eye. Does that sound like something you would like to do?"

"Yes. That sounds perfect." Charlotte scooted forward on the sofa to stand, but the woman had more questions. "When is the wedding and what sort of venue are you holding it in?"

"We haven't set a date yet. And we haven't chosen a venue."

The woman seemed startled. "Do you have an approximate date?"

"Well," Charlotte said, "I've always thought it's especially romantic to have a wedding either during the Christmas season or around Valentine's Day."

Camille clapped her hands gleefully. "Perfect. It's best to allow six months to have the dress made. We have about six months until Christmas and even more time if you choose Valentine's Day. Now, as to the reason for knowing the venue, that helps us choose the style of dress, the formality of it. A beach wedding dress is generally more casual than one for a wedding in a large church. Do you see what I mean?" She leaned forward expectantly, clearly certain that the bride would be excited to share her plans and her dreams for the wedding.

"I don't believe it would be on a beach." She looked over at Jake's grandmother to see if she had any comments.

"No, I believe my grandson is too formal for a beach wedding. I think he's more of a large church wedding type. Don't you agree, Charlotte?"

She considered that. "Yes. Let's say that the wedding will be held in a more formal setting like a church. Does that help?"

"Very much. And the budget we need to consider?"

Shirley jumped in. "Whatever she wants is fine."

Camille's smile widened. "I can now do an excellent job helping you choose the wedding dress of your dreams. Today." She stood and Charlotte rose to her feet.

Shirley walked with them as they browsed through wedding dresses—dozens, maybe hundreds of wedding dresses. Charlotte still wasn't sure how to get out of this mess. Then the vision of a plan dangled from a hanger in front of her. It was quite possibly the ugliest dress she had ever seen in her life. Now, it might look good on someone, but Charlotte knew with absolute certainty that the someone wasn't her. She pointed to it and said, "I want to try that one on."

Camille picked up the dress without any comment, and they moved on to look at other dresses. Charlotte skipped every beautiful dress, and there were quite a few of them, settling only on dresses she thought would be better suited to a shorter, taller, thinner, whatever woman.

To Shirley, Camille said, "We'll get some dresses on your granddaughter-to-be and have her out here in a short time. You can relax on the couch while Charlotte tries the first one on."

When they were in the dressing room and seated, Camille leaned forward and said, "Okay, who are you? I only get the *no red-carpet dress, please* comment when the woman has been *on* a red carpet." She clearly knew her business.

"Okay, can you keep a secret?"

She nodded vigorously, and Charlotte believed her. Many secrets must be shared while wedding dress shopping.

"My name is Charlotte McDaniel, but I'm better known in music circles as Carly Daniels."

Camille's eyes grew wide. She leaned back and gave Charlotte a long stare. Then she nodded. "I do follow country music. And of course 'Sunshine Cowboy' is one of my favorite songs. I won't ask why you're hiding. But I do need to know, does the older lady here with you know who you really are?"

"No, she doesn't. I'm just her grandson's fiancée."

Camille stood and put her hands on her hips. "There must be some story behind this. But it's none of my business. Let's find you a dress you love." She brought in the first one.

Charlotte felt a little guilty for taking up Camille's time with no intention of buying. She hoped Jake would bring his future bride to this shop so they could make up for today. She didn't want to even ponder the fact that he would marry someone else, though. For now, she was his fiancée, fake or not, and she was going to enjoy the time with him and his family.

Camille slid Ugly Dress #1 over Charlotte's head and fastened it in the back before turning her around to face the mirror. Charlotte grimaced and stepped back as soon as she saw her image.

Camille made a *tsk tsk* sound. "It may not be your best fashion profile."

"No, let's get this thing off."

They moved on to Ugly Dress #2, then #3 and #4. All of them were exactly as she had hoped. They were so bad that Camille didn't even want her to leave the dressing room. By now, she was showing frustration, clearly sensing she was about to lose the sale.

This time, when she left the room, instead of returning with the fifth dress Charlotte had chosen, she brought back a beautiful dress. It had tiny pearls scattered over it, and was shaped to hug her upper body down to her hips, then flare out with layers of sheer chiffon. It was nothing short of gorgeous. And Charlotte had a feeling it would be stunning on her.

As she was about to tell Camille no, this wasn't the dress for her, please bring in the other one and they could wrap up the day, a small tap on the door sounded. Charlotte opened it, and Shirley pushed her face in the crack. Charlotte opened it wider. "Shirley, what are you doing in here?"

"I came to see what was going on. I was concerned. You haven't come out in any of the dresses."

A flaw in her plan. Shirley wanted to see Jake's fiancée in

a beautiful wedding dress. And she'd let her down.

"None of them have looked right on me. We didn't want to show you any of them."

Shirley spotted the dress hanging on the hook on the wall and hurried over to it. "That's beautiful," she gushed as she touched the fabric. "Oh my goodness, this is so pretty. Try this one on for me, Charlotte?"

So that was how Charlotte ended up trying on the kind of dress she'd wanted to avoid.

And then she saw it in the mirror.

Her breath hitched.

"You're having a bridal moment, aren't you?" Camille said.

Charlotte nodded. "I watch the bridal dress shopping shows. It always looks like a setup. That doesn't really happen to grown women. And yet here I am, and I want to cry because I'm wearing this dress. I want Shirley to love it too."

She walked down the hall to where Shirley was again seated, feeling like royalty. Like a princess. Like someone who Jake would want to see walking down the aisle. Tears would come to his eyes because she was so beautiful. She reached the area where they'd first been seated and stood in front of Shirley.

Shirley put her hands on her cheeks and sighed. "Let me see the back, please."

Charlotte did as she'd asked, then turned back to face her.

"Can we see it with a veil, please?"

Camille gave a knowing smile. "Of course we can. This is the fun part. You get to see what she'll look like as a bride."

Now sad tears began to prick Charlotte's eyes. She didn't want to hurt Shirley. She didn't want to hurt any of these people. How had she gotten here? It was so simple in the beginning. She needed a job. He needed a housekeeper. Then one kiss and she was *engaged*.

Camille and an assistant twirled and pinned her hair into an updo, then added a veil. This time when Charlotte turned to face the mirror, an amazingly beautiful bride stared back at her. It was exactly how she wanted to look on her wedding day.

"We'll take the dress," Shirley said. "Won't we, Charlotte?"

She nodded slowly. She couldn't say no to this woman. If this made her happy, then that was fine. Maybe Jake would still be able to cancel the order when they ended their relationship.

Charlotte left the shop in a daze, sliding sunglasses on as she stepped out the door. It wasn't that she wasn't familiar with both having and spending quite a bit of money, but never ever someone else's money and under false pretenses. But she couldn't get the vision of herself wearing that dress out of her mind. She wished Jake could see her in it, just once, because it was so beautiful.

Just a few feet from the limousine, motion to her left caused her to turn. A man with a camera was snapping photos of her. She stopped, stunned. It had been a beautiful dream, but she must have been discovered.

"Is Jake Anderson getting married?" the man asked.

Not her, Jake.

Before Charlotte could say anything, Shirley stepped between them. "Leave. My grandson's love life is none of your business."

The man grinned and took a photo of Shirley.

The little firebrand had just confirmed Jake's name, and that Charlotte was part of his love life.

CHAPTER FIFTEEN

*T*hat night Charlotte put on pajamas, which she thought was the best plan after the little escapade with Jake while she was wearing her sleep T-shirt. That had led to a kiss, then to a fake engagement, a wedding dress, and to her falling more and more for him. No more sleeping in T-shirts—maybe forever, but definitely not as long as she was living in this house.

The evening had ended much less eventfully than previous ones. Jake had messaged both of them that afternoon about a dinner meeting he'd forgotten to mention, so she hadn't been able to explain about the dress. Marta had served her and Shirley a lovely meal, but she'd missed Jake. Having dinner with him had quickly—too quickly—become an expected part of her life.

Charlotte slipped under the covers and stared at the ceiling. After a while, she flopped onto her right side, then her left. When sleep didn't come, she decided that getting a snack sounded like a good plan.

Finding her dream wedding dress excited her. Finding it when she was fake engaged left her awake at midnight.

She opened the door slowly. No one in the kitchen. She darted over to the refrigerator. Fruit and cheese would make a perfect snack. She fixed a plate for herself, put everything back, then, as she closed the door to the fridge, heard what sounded like someone moving around beyond the kitchen. She froze. Was Jake coming? His grandmother she could take. But Jake and her alone at night in the kitchen had bad idea written all over it.

Of course, when she remembered that kiss? She would like to have an encore of that. She could feel his lips on hers and her melting into his arms, him deepening the kiss, her breath hitching higher. No. She shook herself. The best plan for survival was to stay away from that, to just see this as a gig she needed to get through. One where she got to stay in better quarters than she'd had at the motel.

When she went back to her room with her snack, she checked her purse for her phone, but it wasn't there. Charlotte whirled around toward the kitchen door. She stayed in her area at night. What if Shirley caught her somewhere else in the house at night? She'd put two and two together and get five.

She set her snack on the island and headed into the living area. She whispered, "Where are you? I know you're here somewhere."

A chuckle came from somewhere to her left.

Charlotte froze. "Jake, I hope that's you because that sounded like a very male chuckle."

"Over here," he said from the other side of the room.

She had never paid much attention to the upholstered

chair and small table with a lamp tucked into a corner. Jake sat there now with a book lying open on his lap.

"I lost my phone."

"I wondered who you were looking for."

Looking up the stairs, she said, "I should have left it until morning."

He shrugged. "As my fiancée, you have the run of the house day or night."

"I just thought . . ." She gestured toward the stairs. "If she found us together at night . . . "

"Only if we were caught in a compromising situation." The moment he said those words, he winced. "Not that we would be in one."

"I understand." He had no real interest in her. She wandered around the room checking for her phone. "Not here."

Jake picked his phone up off of the table beside him and swiped across it. Seconds later, a muffled phone ring came from the couch. She dug behind the cushions. "Got it!" She held up her phone.

"Would you like to play a game?" he asked.

Charlotte eyed him. What was he asking? Something sexy would be a no.

He shook his head from side to side, and stood, knocking his book to the floor. "I meant a board game. I suspect you had other ideas." He raised one eyebrow and watched her.

She could feel the heat rushing up into her face. "What did you have in mind, big fella?"

He chuckled. "Monopoly is a possibility."

She shook her head. "Takes too long. Not my favorite."

"Why don't you come over here and check the game closet?

When my family visits, we often sit around and play games. There are plenty to choose from." He walked over and opened a door in the wall of cabinets that also concealed the TV.

She browsed through the games and pointed to one that said it would work for two players. "Is this one good?"

He slid it out of the stack of games. "One of my favorites. Should we sit at the dining table or side by side on the couch with the game set up on the coffee table?"

She felt like he was giving her an out so they didn't have to sit near each other. The dining table was a good idea. But she went with her heart. "Couch."

He studied her as if he was trying to figure her out.

She hurried to add, "It looks quite comfortable to sit on for the amount of time that it will take to play a game, doesn't it?"

He nodded slowly. "Yes, it does."

Charlotte sat on the couch first. When Jake sat, she could feel the weight shift on the cushion, pulling her toward him. And that was exactly where she wanted to be.

As he set up the game, she said, "I'm sorry about the bridal shop and the photographer today."

He sighed. "Not your fault."

"Your grandmother was magnificent."

He chuckled. "She would defend us to the end. I do assume that photo will end up on a website or in a magazine."

"I know. Let's forget about it and just play the game."

He explained the rules, which she tried to focus on. Her stomach growled. "I fixed a snack." She stood, went to the kitchen, and brought it back. The next half hour passed by with her trying to focus on the game but failing miserably. She finally yawned. "I'm exhausted. I'll say you won."

He watched her. "I'd like that." As she walked away, she thought she heard Jake say, "I'd like to think I understood the rules."

It did feel like they were moving pieces around on a game board. She wanted someone to hand her the rules too. Unfortunately, they'd become part of a tangled game of love that the public might now be invited to join.

The rest of the week passed by in a blur. He worked, Charlotte cleaned, and his grandmother spent most of the time in her sitting room. Charlotte had stated concerns about Grandma spending so much time alone, but also that whenever she checked on her, she'd been on her phone or her computer.

Every evening, they ate one of Marta's mouthwatering meals.

The situation changed when they were driving home from church on Sunday.

"You and Charlotte aren't spending enough time together," Shirley said.

Jake glanced in the rearview mirror at Charlotte, who stayed silent. It was up to him to respond. "Grandma, we believe we are."

She shook her head. "You need more PDA."

Charlotte chuckled and he fought a grin.

"Public displays of affection may not be our—"

"Jake, I was married for fifty-one years. Believe me, I know about romance. Your grandfather was the king of romance."

Charlotte grinned from ear to ear. When he raised an

eyebrow and stared at her, she said, "Shirley, Jake and I prefer to keep our romance private."

"Nonsense. You have to at least hold hands." She gave a long look first to Jake and then over her shoulder to Charlotte. "But I'm not talking about hanky-panky. None of that before marriage." She waved her hand in front of her face.

Charlotte coughed and covered her mouth with her hand, but her smiling eyes gave her away.

"Do you have any other suggestions, Grandma?" He knew she did, or she wouldn't have said anything.

"Now that you've asked, I do." His grandmother smiled a little too sweetly. "Marta has prepared a picnic lunch for you. I went online, and it looks like the lawn beside Lake Watauga in Centennial Park is a great place for a picnic."

Charlotte grinned. "That's kind of you, Shirley. It's pretty there, and that's a nice way to spend a Sunday afternoon."

"And, Jake, remember to show her you care in public. Let the world know that you love her."

He felt a twinge near his heart. Love had never entered into this. Right?

Charlotte waited as Jake hefted the picnic basket out of the rear of his red Range Rover in the Centennial Park parking lot. Then he stepped back and closed the hatch.

The Parthenon, a full-scale copy of the Greek building and a remnant from a long-ago event, sat beside them. When he turned toward the lawn and the lake just beyond the parking lot, he shifted the basket to his left side and held out his right hand.

"She's going to ask, and I won't lie to her."

"Okay." Charlotte took his hand, and warmth spread through him. *Ignore it, Anderson.*

She spoke, probably to fill what had become a nervous moment. "It doesn't appear to be overly busy here today."

Jake scanned the area as he loosely held her hand, meeting his grandmother's request but not exactly as she'd intended. "No. I think we'll have our pick of spots."

When they reached the lawn, he led them to an area behind a large tree. Then he released her hand and spread out the plaid blanket Marta had packed. "Let's get everything set up and take some photos."

How had his grandmother done it? Here he was about to sit on a blanket in the middle of a park—in a very public location—to eat lunch with his housekeeper. He glanced at Charlotte as they both sat down. But she'd become more than that, more like a friend. She seemed to be enjoying herself.

"Do you want to sit and enjoy the view for a while, or eat, Jake?" she asked.

She'd always called him by his first name. Maybe she'd always been more of a friend.

"Let's eat. We'll take pictures and then head back. Grandma will be happy."

The light went out of her eyes. She'd been having fun until that moment. He had to make sure, though, that she remembered he hadn't chosen this. His grandmother had gotten them into this situation. Again.

"Lunch is . . . interesting," she said as she started removing containers from the basket.

Jake leaned over to see. "Please tell me you mean 'interesting' in a good way."

Charlotte wrinkled her nose as she continued unloading the basket. "That depends on whether or not you enjoy caviar, foie gras, oysters—"

"Maybe every once in a while when it's served at an event. But for lunch?"

"Umm. Maybe Marta thought we'd enjoy this."

He flopped back on the blanket. "No. This is pure Shirley Miller."

Charlotte crunched on one of the crackers that must have been provided to eat with the foie gras. "Because?"

"She tells me, often, that I don't act like a billionaire. I suspect that she wanted to impress you with my wealth."

Charlotte stretched out, the leaves on the canopy of trees over them swaying in a gentle breeze.

He rolled on his side to face her. "Are you impressed?"

"With your money?" She moved her hand from side to side. "It's okay."

Laughing, he asked, "If billionaire status doesn't impress you, what would?" He needed to remove money from the equation, so he could be certain that she wasn't spending time with him because she wanted her fifty thousand dollars.

"Right now? Fried chicken. Maybe potato salad. Definitely a brownie."

Guitar strumming came from nearby, and they both turned that direction. The slow beat had a romantic sound to it.

"You don't think my grandmother hired musicians, do you?"

The song changed tempo becoming more upbeat.

Charlotte shook her head. "No, I think someone's practicing his or her guitar-playing in the park."

He laughed. "It's nice to have entertainment." Glancing at

the food, he added, "I wish I could say the food looked delicious."

Charlotte looked over to a family walking on the nearby path. "As you said, we're here for a reason. Ask one of them to take a photo of us together so we can show it to your grandmother."

He jumped to his feet. "Let's make her happy."

A minute later, the dad from the family held Jake's phone for a photo while the two of them sat next to each other on the blanket. Charlotte whispered, "Jake, I think we need to sit closer. Remember that she sent us here for more PDA."

He chuckled and put his arm around her shoulders, pulling her nearer. Holding her close was easy. He leaned over to kiss her as the man snapped images of them. *Mistake, Anderson.* She deepened the kiss, and he wrapped his arms around her.

"Here's your phone."

The words worked through his brain and he realized where they were. He stared into Charlotte's eyes as he pulled away.

When he took his phone from the man's outstretched hand, Jake asked him, "Would your family like a lunch basket filled with goodies like fois gras and oysters?"

The man laughed. "Not a chance. Enjoy it." The family continued down the path toward the lake.

Jake scooped everything into the basket and stood, and Charlotte rose to her feet with a question in her eyes. He reached down, grabbed the blanket, and handed it to her. "Follow me. I have a plan." He headed toward the Parthenon, the place with the most people. When they got there, he loudly said, "I have a basket filled with gourmet foods. I don't enjoy oysters and caviar. If you do, this is yours." He held the basket up high.

A young couple hurried over, and the man said, "If you're serious, we'll take it."

He handed it to them. "I'm serious. We're going for fried chicken." He grabbed Charlotte's hand, and they headed back to the parking lot.

Charlotte played maid again the next day. She cleaned the house from top to bottom while Jake worked, and his grandmother spent the day in her sitting room. As to Jake, she both wished she could see him and was glad she hadn't, because then she'd have to examine her emotions about her boss.

She liked him more than she'd expected to. Knowing a man was easy on the eyes was one thing. Wanting to spend every waking moment with him was another.

As she relaxed on the couch in the screened-in porch that afternoon, a new song came to her, one that made her heart sing.

The song was about love and the heart.

She gasped. "It's about Jake!" She'd gone and done the one thing she wasn't going to do. She'd fallen in love with Jake Anderson.

The picnic had turned into a day she'd remember. The kiss. Wow. They'd followed that with a laughter-filled lunch. Then he brought her home, and they returned to boss and employee.

Now Shirley opened the porch door wearing a big grin on her face.

"I have a surprise for you and my grandson. You're going to dinner tonight with him."

Charlotte waved her hand in front of her. "Thank you, Shirley, but I'm planning to stay here tonight."

Shirley got a determined expression on her face. "You need to spend time alone with your fiancé."

How could Charlotte argue with that? Shirley believed they were engaged. She smiled. "Then we'll go."

She clapped her hands with glee. "I texted Jake. Your reservations are for seven. He's coming home early."

CHAPTER SIXTEEN

*C*harlotte went to her closet and had the easy choice of pulling out the one dinner-worthy dress she had, the one Maggie had made her take. The idea of a place to wear it had felt laughable, but her life had improved in the short time since then. A handsome billionaire—more importantly, a really kind man—was taking her to dinner. She'd go all out for him.

She slipped the dress on over her head, then did the classic single woman's dance of tugging the zipper up from the bottom, trying to reach and pull it from the top, pushing from the bottom and, finally, being able to reach it and tug the thing up. She shook out her arms.

She'd forget about everything else and just have fun. In the bathroom, she searched through her makeup, digging deeper beyond the girl-next-door makeup she'd been wearing lately to the darker tones she used to wear all the time. Tonight called for a sultry, smoky look.

With a practiced hand, she put on her makeup, finishing

with deep pink on her lips. Then she fluffed her hair and stood back.

The dress was beautiful. She had perfect makeup. She'd even grabbed the sparkly evening bag. "Jake Anderson, you won't know what hit you."

Hand on the doorknob, Charlotte looked down. She had bare feet. Worse than that, she didn't have any dressy shoes. She'd left all of them behind along with her former life, and now what would she do? She went over to her closet to sort that out.

She wasn't sure what she'd expected to see—maybe a fairy godmother about to hand her a glass slipper or two? The only sparkle in her walk-in closet came from the glass door pulls on the drawers.

She did find sneakers, cheap flip-flops, and hot pink cowboy boots. She stared at the boots. It had been a while since she'd worn them. Sitting on the upholstered chair, she slipped on first one boot, then the other, and stood.

When she stepped back and saw herself in the full-length mirror leaning against the wall, she thought, *I'm back. Carly Daniels is back.* She didn't have everything her old life had included, though. Then again, she enjoyed pieces of her new life.

Then light burst through the clouds, and she realized she didn't want to be Carly Daniels anymore. She might not even want a comeback as a country music star. She just wanted a great life, a happy life. And she'd really like that life to include Jake Anderson.

If she could occasionally sing on a stage, that would be the cherry on top of the sundae. But for the first time in years, she felt like singing wasn't the most important thing.

Her career wasn't the thing that trumped everything else in her life.

She loved Jake and liked his grandmother. They were great people. She hoped she got to keep them in her life.

No more would there be friends who were only with her because of what she could give them, or because of who they thought she was or who they thought she *should* be. Jake and Shirley had accepted her when they thought she was a destitute housekeeper. They weren't groupies, and they weren't competitors waiting to see what they could get from her.

Spinning, the dress twirled around her. Tonight held promise. She closed the door securely behind her to make sure that her little scalawag didn't escape.

Jake stood when she entered the living area. When she came closer, his jaw dropped.

"Charlotte?"

She giggled and spun once for him. "Do I clean up well?"

He took a step toward her, then paused. "You're beautiful. Stunning!" He glanced around, then pulled a check out of his coat pocket. "I know I said I'd give you this when my grandmother left, but I want to give it to you early. Take it before Grandma gets here." He put it in her outstretched hand.

She rolled it up so she could tuck it into her evening bag. This money meant freedom. She could choose her future now.

The doors on the elevator opened, and Shirley stepped out. "Charlotte, how pretty you are. And only in Nashville would you find cowboy boots with a little black dress."

Charlotte laughed. "That's true." She didn't share her limited options.

Shirley shooed them away with her hands. "It's time for you two to get going. Go have fun."

"Grandma, do you have a man coming over here to meet you?" Jake teased. "You seem to want us out of here in a hurry."

His grandmother laughed. Then she motioned with her hands again to get them on their way.

"Okay, okay. I know when someone wants me out of the house." He turned toward Charlotte. "Are you ready to go?"

"Where are we going?"

"Oh yes," his grandmother said as she reached into her pocket, pulling out an envelope. "This is the gift certificate for the restaurant you're going to tonight. I included enough so that you can stay for dessert." She winked at him." She wasn't sure what the wink meant coming from his grandmother, and she didn't want to spend too much time thinking about it.

As Jake opened the envelope, Charlotte leaned over to look too. The generous amount could feed a family at the best restaurant in town.

"Wow, Grandma! Are you sure that this is what you want to do?"

"You two young people just have fun. The old folks will just relax here on the couch. Maybe I can find a game show on TV. I think I saw some pudding in the fridge too."

They might have to bring her dessert.

Jake stared at his grandmother for a minute, then put his arm on Charlotte's back and directed her out the door and into the car.

As he backed up the car, he said, "That was a very strange conversation we just had with my grandmother."

Charlotte fumbled nervously with her hands, almost like she was trying to figure out what to do with them. She looked up at him. "What do you mean? She seemed to be feeling fine and happy."

"Are you kidding? Game shows and pudding?"

Charlotte chuckled. "You're right. Your grandmother seems more like an action movie and latte kind of woman."

"Absolutely! When we get home, I need to find out what's going on."

Charlotte leaned back in her seat and focused straight ahead as she spoke. "Jake, this might be a good time for us to learn about each other. I know you're my boss, but we're having dinner out, and you're my fake fiancé. I need details."

"What do you want to know? I'm handsome and clearly have a way with the ladies." He put on his best movie star smile.

Charlotte giggled. That was exactly what he was hoping for.

"Let's just relax and try to be friends tonight. Because," he smiled, "I wouldn't want to marry someone I didn't see as my friend."

"Were you friends with Evangeline?" She held up her hand. "Never mind. None of my business."

Jake didn't want to talk about Evangeline, but he may as well get this conversation out of the way. "She was a beautiful woman with a winning smile."

"I don't need to hear more. It's just that I watched the video—"

"Has everyone on earth watched that video? Will the humiliation never end?" Then he realized he *only* felt humiliation. Had it always been that way? Had his heart never been connected to that breakup moment? He sat back in his seat, keeping his eyes focused on the road. He hadn't loved Evangeline. He'd loved the idea of Evangeline and happily ever after.

"Jake? Are you okay? I am sorry that I brought her up."

He reached out and patted Charlotte's hand. Then he grabbed it snugly in his own and squeezed gently. "I've never been better. Evangeline was a model who had graced the cover of many magazines. She was famous, and I felt good being with her, but I think it was in the way that a commoner feels next to royalty—almost as though the glamour will rub off on them, that they'll become something more special than what they were to begin with."

Silence greeted him. Had he somehow offended her?

Then she spoke. "I understand better than you can imagine. There's something about being around celebrities. It's like a magnet for some people. They want to be close to them, and I'm not even sure why. Why do they think that one person is so much more special than another? It's stifling and it's wonderful, all wrapped up in one." Then she seemed to shake herself and laughed in a self-effacing way. "At least that's what I assume it must be like. It certainly feels like that when you see the tabloids at the grocery store checkout, doesn't it?"

The pressure of her hand on his increased, showing stress about the conversation and making him wonder even more about her. Whatever this woman had been through seemed to be somehow tied up with famous people. In this city, and considering the little he knew about her, she must've gotten close to some people who were high up in the music industry.

"Changing the subject to something more fun, what's your favorite flavor of ice cream?" he asked.

"Ice cream?"

He shrugged. "Sure. Let's talk about ice cream."

As they drove under the lights of the restaurant's entrance and valet parking, he could see the smile that lit Charlotte's face.

"Ice cream it is."

He pulled in behind another car with a couple who stepped out and handed the parking attendant the keys. While they waited, Charlotte said, "I'm more of a fruity ice cream kind of girl. Though fudge swirl works for me pretty well too. How about you?"

This woman could make just about anything fun. "I'm into ice cream with stuff in it: old-fashioned Rocky Road with nuts and marshmallows, maybe mint chip." As the other car moved, he pulled ahead. Before Charlotte could open her door, he hurried around the car to open it for her.

She stepped out in her cowboy boots and her hot little dress. She wasn't famous, but she carried herself well, and that was one of the things that made her more special.

As they stood there, Charlotte glanced around and did the oddest thing by pulling out her sunglasses and slipping them on.

"And you just put those on," he pointed to the glasses, "because?"

She hesitated. He sensed that she didn't want to tell him something. "Good question." At that moment, the man handed Jake the ticket to retrieve his car later, and she turned to go inside without giving an answer.

When they entered the restaurant, he knew that his grandmother had done a great job in choosing. Knowing her, she'd checked restaurant review sites online and found the high-end ones that had what she wanted.

"Jake, it's beautiful! White tablecloths, candlelight, and designed so each table has privacy." Charlotte glanced around as they sat down, then took off the sunglasses and tucked them back in their case in her purse. Stranger and stranger.

Their table for two sat tucked in a corner. It was elegant, and very Nashville, with comfortable chairs that combined russet red velvet and rustic wood. A kind of high-class edgy. Sometimes people called Nashville NashVegas, but that really only applied to a few areas of it. Nashville had a vibe all its own. Comfortable and cool as opposed to shiny and glitzy. Not that you couldn't find that here. You could find just about anything.

Her eyes sparkled as she looked at the bottom of the menu. "We'll have dessert later," she said, very slow and sultry. Then she laughed and added, "I mean ice cream, of course." She winked at him.

Jake laughed so loudly that people around them stared. This woman was something special.

Charlotte raised the menu in front of her face.

"Is there something you're trying to read?"

"The light is rather dim in here." She peered over the top of the menu, then lowered it. Smiling, she added, "I think I'll have the salmon. How about you?"

First his grandmother had acted oddly, and now Charlotte. But when she smiled normally, he thought maybe the up-close menu wasn't weird. Maybe it *was* dim on her side of the table. He gave the menu another glance then closed it, saying, "Steak."

"Don't tell me you're a steak and potatoes kind of guy when you go to restaurants? No imagination?"

He opened the menu up again. "I do tend to get a steak everywhere I go. Maybe you should push me outside of my comfort zone."

"Considering the happy expressions everyone in this restaurant has, I would say that you're going to get an awesome steak, so don't let me push you in the wrong direction."

He considered the shrimp scampi, but he knew there was a lot of garlic on that, and he had plans for kissing Charlotte when they got back to the house.

He hoped he was reading her as well as he thought he was. She did not seem like his housekeeper. Then again, she never really had. Tonight, she was a beautiful woman spending the evening with him. The server brought them warm bread and introduced himself and suggested several appetizers.

"I think your grandmother would be disappointed if we returned too quickly, Jake," Charlotte said. "I think we'd better go for several courses."

"You're right." He chose an appetizer, they ordered their entrees, and the man left.

"So tell me about your childhood, Charlotte McDaniel."

A happy expression lit Charlotte's face. "I had a great childhood. We had fun. We lived in Southern California, and we often went to the beach. I'm an only child."

He picked up the napkin sitting beside his plate and spread it on his lap. "And when did you move to Nashville?"

"I'd just turned fifteen. My parents thought Nashville was a city filled with opportunity. So we packed up everything that would fit in a rental truck, sold or gave away the rest, and put the car on a trailer, and drove across the country to begin a new life here."

"And was it a city filled with opportunity?"

"It was that. It still is."

"And your parents? You don't seem to have anyone else around."

"They were killed in a plane crash about five years ago."

He reached out and grabbed her hand. "I'm so sorry, Charlotte. I didn't mean to bring up an old wound."

She shook her head. "It's okay. A lot of time has passed since then. The worst thing about it was that we'd become estranged. And it was all about money."

He thought he heard her add, "Money and fame," under her breath. But whose fame? Maybe her mother or father had wanted to become a music star. It seemed like every day a busload of hopefuls arrived in Nashville, with stars in their eyes.

She gave a smile that didn't reach her eyes. "But I don't want to ruin our evening. I had a wonderful childhood. Let's leave it at that." She looked up from a buttered slice of bread. "I do have my best friend Maggie in Seattle. She's the only one who knows about us." Then she changed subjects. "Tell me about your childhood, Jake. I imagine you've got a fairly happy story to share."

"I do. I had a happy childhood."

"Played sports?"

"High school football quarterback. And I was on track and field and played a bit of baseball."

"Where did you grow up? Your grandmother lives in Florida."

"Not there. That's where she moved when she retired. I grew up in Montana."

She rested her elbow on the table and leaned her head on her hand. "Am I looking at an honest-to-goodness cowboy?"

He grinned. "You would not want to see me on a horse."

She grinned wider. "From the sounds of it, I think I would. Bad?"

"I don't know how to rope, and I've never been in a rodeo."

She kept smiling. There was something addictive about this woman's smile. He'd like to do everything he could to keep it going all night long and into tomorrow.

She held up her hand and ticked off on her fingers. "Okay. So good early childhood, high school jock, and played sports in college?"

"No, ma'am. In college, I was all about business. Once I had my degree in architecture, I went on for an MBA. When I got into flipping properties, I passed the real estate exam, so I'm also a real estate agent."

Their appetizer came, and they each took a bite. Then he picked up his glass of water. "What about you, Charlotte? College? What did you major in?"

"I went to work right out of high school. I actually went to work when I was in high school. And I've been working ever since. I didn't have time for college, and I earned enough that it didn't matter to me. I might like to go back sometime, though, and get a degree."

"In music?" He watched her expression to see what she said. Because part of her mystery was tied up in this. And he wanted to know everything about her.

She glanced away and seemed to find something fascinating on the other side of the restaurant. Then she looked back at him. "Until recently, everything I've done has been in music." She gave a satisfied nod. Then she picked up her water glass and looked at him over the top. "There are times when I wish I had gone to college, and I wonder if I'll find time to go later in life. Not because I need to have a degree, but because I think it might be fun. I'd like to see what I missed and learn new things."

Jake took another bite of the appetizer.

"I'm rather surprised that you would be a calamari kind of guy."

When he looked at her with puzzled eyes, she pointed at the appetizer.

He shrugged and took another bite of it. "I'm usually more steak and baked potato, so I had no idea what it was. When the menu said it was tempura something, I figured it would taste good. You can cover almost anything with batter, deep-fry it, and I'm a happy man. I enjoy the South's passion for frying foods." He bit into the piece again and chewed.

"Squid."

"Excuse me?"

"*Squid,*" she said, with emphasis this time. "That's what calamari is. You just didn't seem like a squid guy."

He stared at the piece of appetizer he had just picked up. He *wasn't* a squid guy. He wasn't a fancy anything with food kind of guy. He popped it in his mouth and chewed. "Thank you for not telling me what it was before I decided that I liked it."

She laughed. "Just like a little kid. Give him a taste, but don't tell him what it is."

By the time their dinner arrived, they were having a great conversation. Jake was glad his grandmother had done this. And he'd started to see why. He and Charlotte never got to have much time alone together. Partly because his grandmother didn't allow it, though. She saw the danger of the two of them being alone in his house. Picnics and dinners were fine.

When their entrées arrived, Charlotte took a bite and closed her eyes in bliss. "This is fabulous salmon."

Jake cut into his steak and tried it. "Perfectly cooked and wonderfully seasoned. I'm going to have to come back to this restaurant."

Charlotte nodded agreement as she took another bite of her dinner. He hoped to return here with her.

When it came time to order dessert, she hesitated.

"You don't want dessert? I'm going with the chocolate chocolate chip ice cream. They say it's a specialty of the house, and it's drizzled with a raspberry sauce."

"I do want dessert. I'm just torn. Do I get the ice cream? The homemade strawberry ice cream sounds fabulous, I must add. Or do I go with a chocolate cake with chocolate frosting and chocolate drizzle?"

"So fruity ice cream versus chocolate?"

She chewed on her lip as she studied the menu.

"I have an idea," he said. "I'm okay with either of those desserts. Actually, I'm okay with any dessert. Let's get the two you want and share them. Deal?"

She gave a slow grin. "Deal!"

When the desserts came, he took the ice cream, and Charlotte took the chocolate cake. He had a bite of his and she of hers. When he reached his spoon into her cake and she put her fork into his ice cream, their eyes met and he gulped.

She slowly brought the fork to her mouth and slid it in and closed her eyes, savoring the bite. What that woman did to him. He took a bite of the cake.

"Fabulous. Both are fabulous." She took another bite of her cake. "Could this night get any better?"

He hoped she'd let him kiss her tonight when they got back to his place. And that would be the frosting on the cake of the evening. He paid for their check with the gift card, and when they were ready to leave, he stood first and pulled out her chair for her.

Standing, she put her hand on his cheek. "Thank you for this evening."

Something in his heart changed at that moment. He couldn't put it into words, but he knew they belonged together. He just needed honesty from her first.

Charlotte looked into Jake's eyes and felt her heart melt. This man. She wanted this man as a forever part of her life. She'd had about ten chances tonight to tell him who she really was. She'd chickened out *every single time*.

Tomorrow, she promised herself. She would figure out a way to tell him tomorrow. And she wouldn't waffle. She wouldn't back down. That was the only way they could have a future together. She might be out on her ear when he found out who she was, and that she'd hidden the truth. But she'd put that check in the bank first thing in the morning, so she could pay for a new place if she had to leave.

She'd started to relax on the drive to the restaurant. When they'd stepped out of the car, she'd looked down, and noticing her boots, realized that tonight, other than the hair color, she was Carly Daniels. Oh, not on the inside anymore, but on the outside—oh yeah. Her makeup and the hot pink cowboy boots. It wouldn't take much for a fan to figure it out. It had looked ridiculous for her to put sunglasses on in the dark, but she'd really wanted this evening to go well, to have a great time with Jake.

In his car driving home, she leaned back in her seat and sighed. "Your grandma did well with this one, didn't she?"

"She did at that. Charlotte, who are you, really?"

She sat upright. "I'm a woman who's had some struggles lately. Can we leave it at that until tomorrow?"

A long silence greeted her. Yes or no, which would it be? He finally said, "I agree to those terms."

"Jake, it isn't a business agreement."

"I think it's best for me to see it that way for now."

She could understand that. Cool. Logical. The heart didn't work that way, but if that was what he needed. They drove in silence on the way home, but it was a pleasant silence. She enjoyed that. Peacefulness with this man, with any man. It felt like she hadn't had a lot of that in her life, at least not for a long time.

CHAPTER SEVENTEEN

*T*hey pulled into the garage, and the headlights illuminated a large sign hanging from the door into the house. Charlotte was surprised by the large sign that read: *A surprise awaits in the backyard.*

Jake and Charlotte looked at each other.

"What do you think she's done now?"

"You know your grandmother far better than I do."

"She loves family. She loves people. I wouldn't be surprised if she had the backyard decorated in a romantic way. Or if there were violins playing."

Charlotte popped open the car door. "Well, there's only one way we're going to find out. After the beautiful evening she's already gifted us, the least we can do is continue with the rest of her surprise."

Before they got out of the car, Jake turned to her. "I'd like to kiss you now, Charlotte. Normally, I would walk the girl to her door and give her a kiss." He brushed the side of her face with his hand. "But not with a grandmother as a chaperone." He'd failed at keeping this all business, and she couldn't be happier.

Charlotte didn't wait for him to kiss her. She leaned toward him, and they met in the middle. The kiss started out sweet and she kept it that way, pulling back after a few seconds.

Every time she thought about a future with him, she came back to the *almost* lies. She had to have a clean slate before they had a chance at a future. And she wasn't sure he would want her once she'd revealed the stack of almost lies.

"Jake, knowing your grandmother, she heard the car pull up."

He chuckled. "You're probably right. Perhaps her surprise is something simple, like pecan pie?"

Charlotte laughed. "Probably. Maybe we could warm it up and put some ice cream on it?"

"Whatever you want, milady."

If only it were true. But she was going to pretend it was for the rest of this evening. She had to come clean. It felt like a train was speeding toward a curve. If she could slow it down before it reached the curve, she might be able to save this whole thing.

They entered the house and walked through the dining room to the French doors leading to the backyard. As they arrived, she put her hand on Jake's arm. "Jake, something doesn't look right. It's your house, but . . ." She shrugged and pointed outside.

"Fairy lights are hanging off the patio cover and scattered around the yard."

"I noticed, but I thought maybe we just hadn't turned those on the other night."

"No, they weren't there. I've never had any. Grandma has been up to more than pecan pie."

He put his arm around her waist, and together they stepped into the backyard. As their feet touched the ground, low lights came on, and a band started to softly play. She giggled. His grandmother had set up a romantic, private scene for them. That was sweet.

Then the lights came on fully, and she saw that it was not private. The backyard must have had a hundred or more people in it. Mitch and Andy were part of a group of four musicians. Chairs were scattered about the periphery of the area. To the right, a long table overflowed with food, including a cake stacked several rounds high that resembled a miniature wedding cake.

The crowd cheered and well wishes resounded from every corner. "Congratulations!" "Never thought I'd see you engaged!" And her least favorite, "When's the wedding?"

Panic swept over her. She leaned toward Jake and whispered, "I think we walked into our own engagement party. What are we going to do?"

He scrubbed his hand down his face. "There's probably no way the media is going to miss this. We suspected the wedding shop photo would be a problem. This is a *definite* problem for our *private, fake* engagement."

Shirley came over and thankfully only caught the last word. "Yes, it's for your engagement! What do you think?" It was hard to challenge the smile on her face. She had gone to a lot of effort to have everyone here.

"Thank you, Grandma." He nudged Charlotte.

"Yes, thank you, Shirley."

As the three of them spoke, the crowd went back to talking amongst themselves.

Charlotte glanced around, knowing she needed to say more. "It's beautiful. I think we can say you surprised us."

She heard Jake mutter, "That's an understatement."

A man and woman in their fifties or sixties stepped forward and Jake hurried over to them. "Mom! Dad! I'm so glad to see you. Was your trip good?"

His dad looked toward Charlotte. "My trip may not have been as good as your time at home. Would you like to introduce your mother and father to the woman in your life? The woman you are apparently planning to marry?"

Charlotte felt like a deer caught in headlights. Jake motioned for her to join them, but she could only stare in shock, so he brought his parents over to her. Standing beside her, he put his arm around her waist and tucked her close. "Charlotte, I'd like for you to meet my dad and mom, Charles and Ruth Anderson."

With their expectant faces, she managed to say, "It's nice to meet you." It would be under normal circumstances. *Nothing* about this was normal.

His mother hugged her and his dad shook her hand. But she wasn't sure this was a happy moment for either of them. They must have been shocked when they learned about their son's engagement.

The band started playing again, this time something a little more country. Charlotte knew it well. If she could get through this party, she could talk to Jake. She'd tell all when the party ended.

She saw people pointing at her cowboy boots. Between her and Jake, and even at the restaurant, she'd probably been okay. But in a group this size, there was bound to be someone who recognized her and confirmed it with her signature boots.

And then a man stepped out from the crowd and held his phone toward them. "Do you have a quote for the media about your engagement, Jake Anderson?" The man beside him snapped a photo of the two of them. Charlotte recognized him as the photographer from outside the bridal store.

"Oh my goodness, Jake!" his grandmother cried. "I did not invite the media to this event."

"Then they're leaving, aren't they?" His menacing tone would send anyone running.

The reporter with the phone held up his hands in surrender. "Okay, okay. I'm leaving." He gave Charlotte a long glance as he walked away with the photographer. She watched him as he reached the edge of the crowd. Then he turned back with his eyes wide, stopped, and stared at her. Busted.

He grinned, patted the photographer on the shoulder, and they raced around the corner of the house.

She turned to Jake. "There's something I need to tell you. You probably should hear it now. And from me."

When his grandmother and others started clapping to the music, she wondered if he'd even heard her.

"I think you'll have to tell me later," he shouted.

Charlotte nodded. The train was sliding off the tracks. Hitting the railing was imminent.

That song ended, and his grandmother said, "I asked them to play upbeat and happy music tonight. It's Nashville, so I thought country would be right, but none of that sad I-lost-my-girl kind of stuff."

They started playing "Sunshine Cowboy," one of the best-known happy songs in country music. As they did, Mitch stopped playing for a beat, then picked back up. He nudged

Andy and nodded with his head over toward Charlotte. Andy looked at Mitch and then back at Charlotte and kept playing, but a look of realization crossed his face. They knew who she was.

Those two guys had been very nice. They were in Nashville to get their big break and actually had quite a bit of talent packed into the two of them. She'd help them get a good start. She may be going down in flames big-time, and this whole wonderful fantasy may be about to end, but somebody could get something good out of it.

"Jake, Charles, Ruth, and Shirley, please excuse me. I can sing, and I think I'll join the band for a song."

"I've heard her sing," Jake said. "She has a beautiful voice."

His grandmother agreed. "I actually heard her singing with those two boys. They sounded great together. Will you be singing that song, Charlotte?"

Jake looked startled at the news that she'd been singing with his gardener.

"Yes, ma'am. One of those boys wrote it, and I think it has a lot of potential to be a hit."

As she walked away, she heard Jake's father ask him, "What does she know about the music industry?"

She caught just the beginning of what Jake said. "I have a feeling she knows quite a bit about . . ."

She hoped she and Jake would be able to put their relationship back together. He was the one she wanted a real engagement with, a real life with.

By the time they'd finished playing her song, she was standing near Mitch and Andy.

Mitch put his hand over his mic. "Are you Carly Daniels? Andy thought you were, but I said, no way was Carly cleaning houses."

Charlotte shrugged. "I was Carly. Once upon a time. Could we sing your song?"

Mitch's eyes sparkled. "Are you kidding? Sing our song with Carly Daniels?"

Andy jumped in. "That would be a yes, anytime, anywhere on this planet."

They got a mic from one of the other singers, and she stood up with them and announced, "I think these two guys you've been listening to have a great future in music. One of them wrote a song that I believe you're going to like. I'm not sure how many of you know anything about country music. Could I see a show of hands?"

About half, maybe a little more, of the guests raised their hands, including Jake's dad.

"Let's do some rocking right now," Charlotte said. She turned to Mitch and Andy. "You ready, guys?"

They had big grins on their faces.

She tapped her foot. "One, two, three."

They started to sing, their three voices blending beautifully. She searched the crowd for Jake and found him standing next to his grandmother. She held his gaze, but he pulled away and looked down.

CHAPTER EIGHTEEN

*a*s Charlotte sang about love with the men, Jake couldn't move, could barely breathe. She mesmerized the crowd and him with her voice. As people got into the song, swaying to the music and clapping in time with the beat, he turned his head and scanned the group.

"That's Carly Daniels!" His father clapped him on the back. "Why didn't you tell us you were engaged to a country music star?"

He softly said, "I didn't know," but his words were drowned out by the music. Charlotte continued through the song, never missing a beat, as his heart broke.

A rousing ovation and calls for "Encore! More! Encore!" came when the song ended. She bowed and the boys followed suit, following the woman that they now knew had been on a stage a time or two.

Into the microphone, she said, "Thank you all. This song was written by these two men, Mitch and Andy. I know you'll hear great things from them in the future. And now I'll leave the rest of the music to them."

Jake heard her name being whispered through the group as she walked back to him. Those who knew who she was, who'd figured it out as she sang, were telling those who hadn't. By the time she was a few feet away from him, he suspected everyone gathered around the pool knew that Jake Anderson's fiancée Charlotte McDaniel was actually country music star Carly Daniels.

The sounds around them faded away when Charlotte reached him where he stood with his family near the house. She stopped in front of him.

He looked her in the eyes. "You lied to me."

His parents and his grandmother stayed near his side.

Keeping her eyes on Jake, she said, "Could I speak to Jake alone?"

"Whatever you need to say can be said in front of them," he replied.

His grandmother, tiny little thing that she was, looked up at him with a fierce expression. "Jake, your fiancée wants to talk to you. Let her explain." She glanced at her daughter and son-in-law and gestured with her head away from them.

They all stepped back, but only about ten feet away. Probably so they could rescue him if he needed it. Everyone else at the party seemed oblivious to the tension.

"Jake, I—"

"Don't say it, Charlotte. Or is that even really your name?"

"My name really is Charlotte. Charlotte McDaniel. Carly Daniels was a name conjured up by my manager a decade ago. What you have seen, what you see right now, this is the real me. I haven't pretended to be anything else. Jake, I don't want us to end."

He shook his head and gave her a disgusted look, anger

starting to take over. "There is no *us,* Charlotte or Carly or whatever. There was just you and me and a fake engagement. And now you will be leaving."

She gasped. Then she slowly tugged off the engagement ring. She reached for his hand, but he jerked it away.

"Hold out your hand, Jake." He stared at the ring and held his hand out. She set the ring on his palm and curled his fingers up around it, giving a gentle squeeze. "Please know that the time I spent with you was the best time of my entire life."

He scoffed. "Do you enjoy lying to men? You probably use that line with every man you do this to."

She wiped away the tears rolling down her cheeks with the back of her hand. Then she reached out and touched his cheek.

"Only you, Jake." She went back into the house.

There went the greatest actress he had ever met. She'd almost, *almost,* had him believing the dream.

His family walked back over, and his mother put her arm around him. "Jake, I'm sorry things turned out this way. You really didn't know that you had a country music star as a housekeeper?"

The ridiculousness of the situation caught his attention for the first time. "No, Mom, I didn't have a clue. I guess that makes me the dumbest man on earth."

"When you first stepped out the door with her, I thought you were the happiest man on earth. The way she looked at you, with love in her eyes, made me think, thank goodness, my son, the man that I have hoped to experience this since the day he was born, has finally found the love of his life. None too soon, I might add."

Jake gave a harsh laugh. "What is it about me, Mom, that

makes women give me back a ring? She's exactly like Evangeline. A video of this will probably go viral too."

"I watched the other video," his mother said.

Jake turned toward her. "What? You too! Talk about a private moment being out there for the public to see. There must be something about me that's not right. Why do I attract public humiliation?"

This time his dad spoke up. "Son, I thought you were bright. I remember when you were in kindergarten, thinking that is the smartest boy in the class. Look how he's learning his letters and how to read so early. And then math, oh my goodness, you took to math. But tonight? Tonight, I'm wondering if you've got even an ounce of the good sense that God gave you."

So now his father, who never said a harsh word, was after him. "Dad, I can't take this right now."

"Jake," his grandmother chimed in, "what this girl did was nothing like what Evangeline did. Evangeline threw the ring at you. *That* made the viral sensation."

Jake groaned and put his face in his hands. Even his grandmother had watched the Evangeline catastrophe video. Viral must mean every human being on earth with access to the Internet.

His grandmother continued. "This girl didn't do that. If this video goes viral, you're going to have people crying and sad. Would you say Charlotte handed the ring back to you in a way that Evangeline would have even considered?"

If it had been anyone but his grandmother asking . . .

"Grandma—"

"Think before you speak, Jake. Think about what just happened. Did she do this in anger?"

He shook his head.

"Did she do it out of spite? Or to make a public spectacle out of you?"

Jake shook his head again.

"Then what would you say was in her heart when she did it?" Jake could see Charlotte standing in front of him now, putting the ring in his hand and closing his fingers around it.

Evangeline cheated on him. She'd lied to him and had been engaged to him for prestige, money, and designer handbags. Charlotte had scrubbed his shower, changed sheets, and turned his all-business, boring life into one filled with laughter and happiness.

She wasn't Evangeline. "Charlotte isn't Evangeline."

"Smart boy." His grandmother patted him on the arm.

His head jerked toward the house. "I need to stop her."

"Go get her, son," his dad said.

At that second, Jake heard Charlotte's beater truck rev up and pull out. He raced around the side of the house, everyone parting for him. When he got there, he could see her truck at the end of the driveway with a turn signal on, waiting as the gate opened.

Only Charlotte would think to put a turn signal on when she was crying and emotional. He ran down the driveway, but she pulled out onto the street and was gone. He'd lost her.

As soon as Charlotte left Jake's property, she pulled over to the side of the street. There was no way she should be driving with tears streaming down her face, barely able to see the road. She stopped in a spot that wasn't terribly well lit. The last thing she wanted was for someone to take a picture of Carly Daniels having a breakdown in her truck. She rolled the window enough to get air and heard footsteps crashing along the road. A runner. Or a stalker or a serial killer? She started to roll the window back up, but a hand reached in.

She screamed, and turned the window crank as fast as she could.

"Charlotte!"

She froze just seconds before slamming Jake's fingers into the window trim.

Should she start the truck and just pull away? Considering the current situation, her emotional state, and his seeming lack of interest in her, that seemed like the best plan. She turned the keys in the ignition, and the old truck came to life.

"Charlotte, please let me talk. Don't leave me."

He had her attention.

"Can we sit and talk? Can I get in your truck and sit beside you?"

The hilarity of the situation, the last two weeks of her life, bubbled up inside her, and she started to laugh.

This time when Jake spoke, he sounded like a wounded male. "I don't think I said anything funny. Just tell me to leave, and I will."

"Jake, there's nowhere for you to sit." She gasped out laughter and pointed to the floor on the passenger side. He couldn't see it in the dark, though.

"I see an empty right side of the seat, Charlotte. I'm just going to walk away now." This time, there was a sob from him. And that sobered her up.

"Oh." A few seconds later, he started to laugh. "What am I going to do with you?"

She had so many ideas for the answer to that one.

"Charlotte, I'd like to work this out."

"Why?" she asked in a way that held no laughter now, only hope. Did this man care about her? Was there hope for them yet?

A crack of lightning lit the sky, followed by thunder. Then there was another lightning bolt and thunder, louder this time, much closer to them than the last.

"Charlotte, I don't want to stand out here and get struck by lightning. Can we go somewhere to talk?"

"Jake, I think you said everything you wanted to say back at your house. I didn't lie to you."

"You didn't tell me the truth, either."

She sighed. "You're right. I didn't give you all the information. And I'm sorry if that caused you embarrassment, humiliation, or any other unpleasant emotions and consequences. "

"There's a coffee shop down at the corner. Would you meet me there?"

"Jake, you have a backyard full of guests at your house."

"Not anymore. No one wants to stand outside when there's a storm coming." He paused. "My mother and grandmother probably moved the party inside, anyway." His tone became pleading. "Charlotte? Please come home."

She stepped out of the truck. "Jake, let's not have this discussion in the street. Let me go, and I'll call you. *Soon*," she added for emphasis.

He took her hand. "Charlotte—or should I call you Carly?"

"Charlotte. My name is Charlotte."

"Charlotte, I don't want to let you go. Please don't leave me."

"I don't want to leave you, but you don't know who I am. You don't know country music. A lot of people are going to start talking about you. They'll be hanging around your house to get a picture of you and me together. On top of that, my last two albums? Big failures. I know now that it's because my manager was skimming money off the top of everything and cutting corners. The contracts weren't even what I thought they were. I trusted him." She waved her hand. "But that doesn't change anything, Jake. You don't *want* to be part of my life."

"Charlotte, I'm considered one of the wealthiest men in Nashville and have been on the cover of more than one magazine as bachelor of the month. People already want to take my picture."

"Have you ever been in the tabloids? You haven't lived until you've seen paparazzi camped at the end of your driveway."

"I don't care, Charlotte. And I don't mean I'm just going to put up with it. *I don't care.* I want you in my life. Please come back with me."

One more bolt of lightning lit the sky, and she could see the sincerity in his face and his eyes before it went dark again.

"What if I go on tour, and I'm on the road for months? How will you feel then?"

He wrapped his arms around her and tugged her toward him. "Will you come home to me?"

She leaned her head on his shoulder. "Always."

"Then I'll be waiting for you." He kissed the top of her head.

She raised her head for a kiss as lightning flashed, putting her hands on his cheeks. "I love you, Jake Anderson."

"And I love you, Charlotte or Carly, whoever you are." He kissed her, gently at first, then deeper.

A drop of rain hit her forehead, then another. She pressed into the kiss, forgetting the rain and the world around them. Then she blinked as water ran down her face.

She broke the kiss but stayed in his arms. Steady rain ran down her face as she tilted her head skyward. Laughing, she said, "I think we're about ten seconds from a downpour."

Jake swung her in his arms. "Let it rain!" Then he set her on her feet again and went down on one knee. "Will you marry me? This time I mean it."

She knelt beside him. "Yes, I'll marry you!"

As he slid the ring back on her finger, the sky opened and rain poured down on them, but Charlotte knew they'd survive this downpour, and any others in the years ahead.

EPILOGUE

"This is a disaster."

Charlotte counted to ten to calm down. Her friend Maggie and Jake's sister Lizzie had joined her on a video call. She was in Chicago on her farewell tour with her old band. Mitch and his group were her warm-up group.

"I'm sure there's a solution." Maggie's determined tone of voice agreed with her words. Her expression didn't.

Charlotte felt like getting up and pacing across the room.

"With your final farewell concert scheduled for right before your wedding, and you marrying a handsome billionaire, having the media interested isn't a surprise." Lizzie added, smiling, "I put in the handsome part because he's my brother."

Charlotte laughed. She and Lizzie had become good friends in the last few months. "Thank you for keeping my focus on that handsome man, not on the ceremony." A helicopter flew overhead, the noise fading when it continued on. But it reminded her that paparazzi might fly over the church during their wedding ceremony.

"You may need to move the wedding," Lizzie said.

"I've thought of that. My fabulous wedding planner Cassie is even hunting for a new location. She tells me she'll find something great." Months of planning would have to be erased. She'd start over with only a wedding dress and a groom. "It would have to be a secret location. And once we tell the guests, how does it stay a secret?" She groaned.

Maggie smiled. "You'll have a wedding to remember, no matter where it is."

Charlotte sat up straighter. "You're right."

"Of course I'm right." She grinned. "Remember, you're marrying the man you love."

"He *is* a great guy." Warmth spread through her. She smiled at her two friends. "Anyone have good news? I could use some."

Lizzie shrugged. "Would it be good news if I told you I've decided to keep the motel for a while? I didn't find a buyer at the price I wanted."

Charlotte laughed. "It doesn't resemble the motel where I met Jake. That is good news."

"I haven't come up with a new name for it, though. I'll do that and order a sign next week."

Charlotte looked at her longtime friend. "Anything new and awesome with you?"

"I'd planned to save this news for later. But remember my mentioning a new job possibility in the law firm? One that would require moving to another state?"

Charlotte nodded.

"I got it!"

"Congratulations! Where are you moving to?"

Her friend looked even happier. "Nashville."

Charlotte stared at her. "You're moving *here*?"

Maggie nodded. "Next month. If you need a lawyer to review any contracts," she glared at her, "I'll be right here."

"I won't need that now that I won't be performing anymore after the farewell concert."

Maggie stayed silent for a minute, then asked, "Are you sure you want to stop performing?"

Lizzie nodded. "I've wondered the same thing. Carly Daniels quitting?"

Charlotte knew it with every fiber of her being. "Absolutely. It's time for a new chapter, and McDaniel Music Consulting is doing well. I signed three new coaching clients this month. I owe Mitch a lot for showing me how much I love helping new musicians learn the ropes."

Her phone signaled a text. She picked it up and saw Jake's name. *I love you.*

She replied, *Love you more.*

"He sent you a message, didn't he?" Maggie asked. "You're glowing."

Charlotte put her hand on her cheek. "Yes. It's the love that matters, isn't it?"

She and Jake *would* get married. Sure, she hoped it would be somewhere wonderful, but the two of them saying "I do" was all that mattered.

Thank you for reading Jake and Carly's story! Don't miss their wedding in RUNAWAY TO ROMANCE, the first book in the Wedding Town romance series. In RUNAWAY TO ROMANCE, wedding planner and runaway bride Cassie meets the town sheriff Greg in Two Hearts, Tennessee. She's planning Carly and Jake's wedding.

ABOUT THE AUTHOR

Writing books that are fun and touch your heart

Cathryn always loved reading. When she was in college, a friend gave her a paper grocery bag filled with old romance novels. She read them, her first romances, and asked for more.

A few years later, she found a romance novel with humor in it. She knew then that she wanted to write a book like that. It wasn't published, but she learned a lot.

After that, she applied her communications degree to writing and publishing hundreds of articles, becoming an award-winning journalist.

But she still wanted to write romances. *Falling for Alaska*, the first book in the Alaska Dream Romances, became her first published romance. There are currently nine books set in her home state of Alaska.

She now lives in Tennessee with her professor husband and adorable calico cat. It isn't surprising that she wanted to write books set there.

If you have kids in your life, she also writes middle grade mysteries as Shannon L. Brown, which start with *The Feather Chase*.

For more books and updates, visit cathrynbrown.com

Made in the USA
Monee, IL
30 April 2024

57731751R00111